Life Styles of the Rich and Aimless . . .

The lights dimmed. A bed with a beautiful, naked girl on it rolled on stage. A curly-haired giant came from behind the curtains, dropped his jock-strap, and joined her.

"Some show," Carter murmured

"You better believe it," replied the brunette at his table.

Carter checked his watch. It was time for his own show. He stood and walked to the stage.

"SIN!" he shouted. "This place is full of sin and you are all sinners!"

NICK CARTER IS IT!

FROM THE NICK CARTER
KILLMASTER SERIES

INVITATION TO DEATH

KILL MASTER

NICK CARTER

J

JOVE BOOKS, NEW YORK

KILLMASTER #246: INVITATION TO DEATH

A Jove Book / published by arrangement with
The Condé Nast Publications, Inc.

PRINTING HISTORY
Jove edition / February 1989

ISBN: 0-515-09923-6

Jove Books are published by The Berkley Publishing Group,
200 Madison Avenue, New York, New York 10016.
The name ''JOVE'' and the ''J'' logo
are trademarks belonging to Jove Publications, Inc.

PRINTED IN THE UNITED STATES OF AMERICA

10 9 8 7 6 5 4 3 2 1

*Dedicated to the men of the
Secret Services of the
United States of America*

ONE

Misty rain made Trafalgar Square gleam in the illumination from the sodium lamps. It partially obscured the top of Nelson's Column and gathered in puddles around the statue's base.

It was midweek, nine in the evening, but traffic was heavy with Christmas shoppers hustling to spend their money. On the Pall Mall side, in front of the National Gallery, a Salvation Army band was playing "Hark, the Herald Angels Sing."

A tall man in a dark Burberry coat, a tweed cap pulled low over his eyes, paused in passing. One hand emerged from the coat and coins clattered in the bucket.

"Bless you, sir."

The man hurried on, the wind whipping rain into his face. Across the square, he moved down Whitehall and paused again, looking back. A newspaper, torn and crumpled, tumbled along the gutter, flapped feebly against his leg, and moved on.

A bus turned out of the square. It made a stop at the north end of the Horse Guard's building, and went on.

The man picked up his pace. At the last moment he sprinted across the wide street, and when the bus stopped at the Cenotaph, he darted on board. As it pulled away from the curb, the man made his way to the very rear seat.

All the way to Bridge Road in the Pimlico section, he darted quick looks out the rear window. Until now, there had been a set, wary look on his face. Now, as he dropped from the bus and walked across Vauxhall Bridge, his features relaxed.

On the south side of the Thames, he turned into Leffler Lane. It was a small street, hardly more than an alley. The buildings were narrow and deep, and all connected. Every third one seemed to be a pub or some kind of nightclub.

At number 221, he stopped. There were double doors without windows. Through them he could hear loud rock music emanating from the interior. A photo in a glass-fronted case full of glossy blow-ups to the right side of the door showed a long-legged blonde in a brief showgirl's costume. She was poised on her toes with her head flung back in rapturous abandon and most of her large breasts bursting from a spangled bra.

His glance climbed the wall over other pictures of other women . . . blondes, brunettes, and redheads, each nearly naked.

Above the door, a sign in garish neon script identified the place as Lola's.

He moved his glance up to the windows of a flat above the club. There was a faint light in one of them.

He pushed open one of the doors and found himself in a tiny lobby. There was a short counter on his left. A dark, scrawny, thin-nosed, middle-aged woman was behind it. Opposite the street door was another door, this one with a padded, red leather surface. It was partly open, and through the opening came a thick sound with a beat to it. Music and laughter and scrambled conversation.

"Are you a member, sir?"

"No."

"Two pound twenty, sir."

The man gave her a five-pound note, pocketed his change, and pushed into the club.

The room was dimly lit. Twenty or thirty tables were scattered across the floor. In one of the far corners, a dais held the band providing music. Its beat was elemental.

The rest of the far wall, and the other corner, was occupied by a long S-shaped bar with a broad plate counter. On top of this counter, greenly illuminated from below and redly from above, six near-naked girls were strutting on high heels, swinging and posturing, smiling blank-eyed, and moving their bodies in time to the primitive beat of the music.

Few of the tables were occupied, mostly by men. Lola's was an after-hours spot. The real moving and shaking wouldn't happen until around midnight.

Behind the bar, a fat, bald-headed man polished glasses, set them down, and picked up others, all without once sparing a glance for what he was doing.

"Whiskey, neat."

When it came, the man dropped a ten-pound note onto the bar and eyeballed the room. Besides the dancers, there were four other women in the room. None of them was Lola.

He remembered the light in the upstairs flat.

The man turned away from the dancers. At the opposite end of the bar he saw an alcove. Just inside, there were two doors to the left and right. At the end, almost in total darkness, was a door marked Private.

"Another, please."

When the drink came, he asked directions for the men's room. The fat man swiveled his head toward the alcove.

He moved past the two rest rooms and tried the private door. It was locked. He took a small ring of keys from his pocket and glanced once over his shoulder.

All eyes were on the exotic dancers.

The second key opened the door. He went through and

relocked it behind him. At the top of the stairs he found himself in a narrow, carpeted corridor softly lit by discreet overhead lights.

A door to his left was marked Office. The one to his right was unmarked and a tiny sliver of light escaped from beneath it. This one he unlocked with a credit card. He opened it only an inch. From somewhere deep in the flat he could hear a shower running.

Smiling, he entered the flat and closed the door behind him.

Soft lights burned in the bedroom, the interior hall, and bath. The heavy plate-glass door to the shower was steamed over, and the moisture made it translucent. Tiny beads of hot water glowed in reds, blues, and greens, while the vapor frosted the door. Behind the door could be seen the moving shadow of a woman.

The sound of the water beating against the tiled walls of the enclosure ceased abruptly and a rounded arm reached from behind the door to pick up a thick bath towel. She stepped from the shower and dried herself.

She gave an impression of height which she did not actually possess. On her head was a shower cap of transparent plastic ornamented with golden snail shells and coral sea horses. When she removed the cap, a mass of blue-black hair tumbled to her shoulders, and she shook her head gracefully from side to side while her hair swirled free. Fresh from the shower, her face devoid of makeup, she had the freshly scrubbed appearance of a young girl.

But she was not a young girl, and the suppleness of her slender body could not conceal her maturity. Her brow, nose, and chin were regular in shape and delicately proportioned, and her small, well-shaped head was balanced on a long, plaint neck which curved gracefully into a swelling bosom.

The width of her face across the cheekbones was wide, and the bones themselves high, with the skin stretched tautly over them. Her eyes were elongated, slanting upward at a noticeable angle toward the outer edges of her temples, and were an unusual and brilliant color of green.

Her mouth was wide and mobile—the upper lip thin, the lower full—and when she smiled it gave the beholder an impression that it concealed amusement. This appearance of innocence mixed with a curious sophistication gave an odd yet most attractive expression to her face.

Her body was lush, full, with darkly tipped breasts, a narrow waist flowing into womanly hips, and a thick mass of black hair at the base of her flat belly.

After drying her body, she hung the towel through a gold-plated ring mounted on the wall, and inserted her feet into a pair of soft slippers.

She entered a dressing room that adjoined the bath. The walls were painted a deep rose that exactly matched the wall-to-wall carpet. A large mirror in a gold and white frame stretched from floor to ceiling and reflected a French baroque dressing table and chaise longue standing across from it.

From the dressing table, she selected an ivory comb and drew it casually through her hair until the fine dark mass fell into gentle waves. Next she sprayed her hair with a mist of perfume, then lightly dusted her naked body with a matching scent of bath powder. Hesitating for a moment, she examined her lips in the mirror, then quickly brushed them with lipstick.

Suddenly she held very still. She smelled tobacco, cigarette smoke.

She didn't smoke.

She moved from the dressing room to the interior hall. It extended the length of the apartment, and from it doors opened to the other rooms. The hall ended at two steps that dropped to the level of the large living room. This room was dark except for the faint glow of a single small lamp, and it was filled with soft muted music from a radio.

At the steps dropping to the living room, she paused to gaze intently across the darkened room. She saw, silhouetted against the large window, the outline of a tall figure peering out into the street below. He wore a dark jacket and dark slacks, and stood with hands clasped behind his back and legs slightly apart. The figure continued to stare into the night, oblivious to her approach, which had been covered by the music.

Cautiously, her hand reached out to a small Italian chest beside her. Her face, and its expression, was concealed by a heavy shadow as she opened the top drawer and quietly groped inside.

When her fingers found and closed over the solid butt of a Beretta automatic, she withdrew it, and, holding it in both hands, pointed it at the figure at the window.

"Put your hands in the air and turn around slowly, very slowly."

The figure turned, but the hands and arms stayed at his sides. Worse, he started moving toward her.

"Stop! I'm warning you, and raise your hands!"

The man kept moving.

"Bloody fool!" she said, and pulled the trigger.

The firing pin clicked on empty. As the man stepped forward, the light reached his shoulders. He raised his hand and opened it. Nestled in his palm was the clip from the Beretta.

Then he took another step and the light fell across his face.

"Hello, Serena. Gained a little weight, haven't you?"

"Nick Carter!" she gasped. "You bloody bastard!"

Lola, alias Serena, was in fact Julie Ashford, and even though her English accent was impeccable, her French and

Italian perfect, and her German acceptable, she was from Cleveland, Ohio.

At sixteen, blessed with a full-blown woman's body and the morals of an alley cat, she had run away to New York City. There she had lied about her age and worked in a fairly high-class strip joint. Six months of that and she had progressed to being a high-class call girl.

Along the way, she met and married a French magician who dabbled in fleecing rich old ladies who wanted to contact their dead husbands. He pimped little Julie on the side until they could set themselves up in style on the East Side of Manhattan.

Everything went fine for a couple of years, until the Frenchman mingled in a little blackmail. When the heat got too heavy, they both ran for his native Paris.

It wasn't long before they were set up again in the same business. For another couple of years everything was dandy. Then a Russian, code-named Choker, got onto their scam and hired them to do a little blackmail for him.

That worked for a while, until Choker found out they were selling to the highest bidder.

The Frenchman bought the farm and was found floating facedown in the Seine. Little Julie took off for London and became Madame Serena.

That was where Carter met her. Together they had upset the apple cart of a crazy religious cult named Pastoria in southern France. In the process, Serena had double-crossed Carter at least a half-dozen times, and twice nearly got him killed.

"What the bloody hell do you want, Carter?"

"I just missed your dry wit and wonderful disposition."

"*Merde!*"

She flipped on an overhead light and, completely oblivious of her nudity, crossed to the bar. Pointedly, she poured a single gin and leaned back, elbows on the bar, to face him.

"I had all of you I could stomach the last time. Get out."

Carter moved around her, grabbed a bottle of Chivas, and poured three fingers in a glass. "As I remember, I could have killed you and didn't."

"Maybe you should have."

"And your last words were, 'Next time,' as I remember."

"I was conning you."

Carter smiled and sipped the Chivas. "I can believe that. I need some help."

"No way. You're poison. You and I have nothing in common anymore. The past is dead, finished. I'm out of the game."

"Are you?"

"Yes," she hissed, but averted her eyes.

"Had a hell of a time finding you, Serena . . ."

"It's Lola now."

Carter shrugged. "All right, Lola, I had a hell of a time finding you. Along the way I found that there's a lot of the old Serena in the new Lola. You ran a jewel scam in Denmark. The jewels came from a lot of expensive flats in Belgravia. With a guy named Huston, you left a paper trail across Spain that would pay off the national debt. And you still dabble in a little blackmail now and then."

She climbed onto one of the stools and shrugged, making her bare breasts do a nice jig. "A girl's got to live."

"Of course. And I'd like to help you along in life."

At this, her green eyes came alive. "Oh? How's your expense account?"

"Healthy."

"Good," she said with a smile, sliding off the stool and bouncing beautifully across the room. "You can tell me about it over dinner!"

TWO

She chose the Chelsea Club, and as Carter followed her following the maître d', he became aware of why she had asked about his expense account.

The restaurant was tastefully plush, without a shred of *nouveau*. The walls were of real burnished oak paneling. The old-style gas lanterns hanging over the tables against the wall were really old, their brass polished to a golden hue. The carpeting was thick and soft as only wool can be. The tables were round, planked, and expertly dressed. The entire room was in soft lantern and candlelight shadow, but not so that one's eyes hurt. Sounds were barely audible, so good was the room's design.

The maître d's tuxedo would roll out at around four hundred dollars, and he wore a Rolex low on his left wrist, below the cuff so it couldn't be missed. He behaved authoritatively rather than obsequiously.

"I am suggesting a table near the wall for you and your guest, mademoiselle. We're expecting a rather sizable crowd tonight. It will be quieter."

"Anything you say, Dominic," Lola purred, flashing Carter a smile.

"Nice joint," Carter growled.

"I like it."

"What if I weren't on an expense account?"

"Then you wouldn't be here." She actually said it without altering her smile.

Every male eye in the place followed their progress. Lola's breasts, *sans* bra, did a wild dance trying to escape the skintight black floor-length gown covering them. The reality of their magnitude was open to inspection, since the front of the dress was cut to her navel.

At the table, Dominic pulled out their chairs one by one. He snapped his fingers and two waiters came floating across to push them back in occupied. One of them stayed to take drink orders.

"I'll have gin over gin," Lola said. "Monsieur will have Chivas, neat. And I believe we will have a plate of shrimp, the lobster pâté, a few oysters, and a little caviar."

"The Beluga, mademoiselle?"

"Is it the most expensive?"

"Oui, mademoiselle."

"The Beluga it is," she replied, and gleamed some teeth at Carter.

"Ah, little Serena, you have changed."

"Please, let's keep it Lola from now on."

Carter returned the smile with clenched teeth. "Lola it is."

The drinks came.

She raised her glass. "To the biggest bastard I've ever met."

"To one of the most beautiful bitches I ever bedded."

She didn't bat an eye. "If you remember, Carter, it was *I* who did the bedding."

She was right. She had attacked him in a villa on the

Côte d'Azur and kept him in bed long enough for someone else to plant a bomb under the driver's seat of his car.

"How can I ever forget," he murmured.

They drank. She dabbed daintily at her crimson lips with a napkin, and leaned forward.

"Now, you were saying?"

"Gerhard Rouse. Ever heard of him?"

Her big green eyes got smaller in concentration. It was several seconds before she answered. "Heard the name. Ran some guns, didn't he? Also took an occasional hit when the price was right?"

Carter nodded. "He became a very wealthy and a very cautious man. He retired about two years ago, to Rio and luxury."

"Hmm, that's something I'd like to do," she mused.

"But you're too greedy," Carter said.

Her eyes flashed, and then she grinned. "You're right. What about Rouse?"

"He free-lanced, but unlike you working both sides, he preferred rubles. That's why we tried to nail him so often."

"But you never did."

"Never," Carter admitted.

Her smile grew broader. "He's a hero to me already."

Carter ignored her. "As long as he stayed in Rio and out of our hair, we left him alone. But about two weeks ago, he surfaced in Madrid. Before we could get anyone on him, he split. One of our people picked him up at the airport in Munich. I was sent in, but he'd already skipped."

"Elusive little shit, isn't he?"

"Very," Carter said, nodding. "I got a line and followed him to Paris. I missed him again, but I found out he put a crew together."

"For what?"

"That's what we want to find out. If Rouse came into the daylight, it was for something very big and worth a great deal of money."

She shrugged and signaled for a new round of drinks. "What's that got to do with me? I don't know Rouse."

Before Carter could reply, the waiter arrived with a new round. Before he left, Lola ordered . . . five courses, and all top of the line.

"And the wine, mademoiselle?"

"You choose," she said, and shooed him away with a flick of her fingers.

Carter shuddered. In a place like this, letting the wine steward make the choice usually resulted in a per-bottle cost of around two hundred dollars.

"Excuse me, Ser . . . Lola, but doesn't the *man* usually do the ordering?"

"Not when he's out with me. Now . . . Rouse."

Carter sighed and got back to business. "He dead-dropped a letter to London two days ago, just before he left Paris. I managed to get to the cutout, but all I could get out of him was a name and address: Nodo, Fourteen Tottenham Court Road."

Her brow furrowed. "It's a dead-drop on this side as well."

Carter nodded. "The back end of a bookie joint. Entrance is through the alley. The box is rented by mail. Just send in your ten quid a week and nobody sees you pick up your mail."

"So all you've got is a contact name, Nodo."

"That's it. I've gone through Scotland Yard, the computers at MI5, and all the contacts they could give me. Rouse has a head start of two days on me, and whatever is going down is going down soon . . . I think."

"So you want me to help you find Nodo?"

Carter grinned. "Since you probably know every lowlife in London, I figure it should be easy for you."

One carefully plucked eyebrow arched. "How easy?"

"A thousand pounds."

"A day," she said, draining her glass.

"You're out of your mind," Carter retorted.

"Okay. Seven-fifty a day and we eat here every night."

"Five hundred and we eat fish and chips."

She made a face. "Six-fifty and I cook."

"Since when do you cook?"

"I don't, but I have a hooker friend who's an absolute gourmet. I call her in on special occasions."

"It's a deal," Carter said, and the food came.

After returning to her place so she could change into something a little more conventional for the work, they hired a cab for the night and went on the hunt.

The first place was a vast, sprawling, after-hours disco in Victoria Dock Road. Every woman in it looked like she should be walking the streets of Soho, and every man looked like he'd just been released from Broadmoor.

"Nice place," Carter commented.

"Just drink your pink lemonade and let me circulate."

She did, for a half hour, and came up empty.

The next joint, Duke's on Rathbone Street, was just as noisy and just as seedy, but there was a better class of people. The guys at Duke's looked like they might throw you in the river *without* cutting your throat first.

This one took even less time.

For the next two hours, the names blurred and Carter saw more of the "Gents" getting rid of the lager he'd consumed than he did the people. Lola did her usual reconnaissance, all the time passing the word that she wanted to get in touch with "Nodo" for business reasons.

Most of it was a dead end, but in one joint she found out Nodo's claim to fame.

"He's a wheel man, one of the best, and evidently he's hot with anything with an engine."

"Where to now?" Carter asked, bleary-eyed.

"We keep moving."

Around three in the morning they hit a place called the Angry Onion. It was a bit smaller than the other places, and far less crowded. Lola maneuvered Carter to the empty end of the bar and two stools.

"So, Lola, luv, what'll ya have?"

"A gin, Glenda, and me mate'll have a pint of yer best bitter."

Glenda was fairly tall, a blonde somewhere in between straw and platinum. Carter guessed she was on the hard side of forty, but she was well preserved. It was her eyes that made him sure she was older than she looked. They had seen all the surprises; there weren't going to be any more.

She set a gin in front of Lola and the bitter before Carter. "There ya are, luv."

Her look took him all in at once with loving appreciation, in the same way a butcher might look at a crown roast.

Carter thumbed his wad to pay, and Lola plucked a twenty-pound note from the top. She pushed it across the counter.

"Keep the change, dearie."

"To what do I owe the generosity?" the blonde murmured.

"I'm lookin' for a lad. They say he's well connected and drives like Sterling Moss."

Glenda's eyes slitted and her mouth got a little hard. "And who might that be?"

"His contact name is Nodo. Do you know him?"

Carter could sense at once that they had hit pay dirt. He

started to peel off another twenty and speak, when Lola's knee crashed against his.

"Nick here would like to do some business with him."

"I know him," Glenda said, "but I ain't seen him around fer nearly six months."

"But you might point us to him?"

"I might."

Again with the knee, and Carter finished the movement peeling off a second twenty.

Glenda smiled as the bill disappeared into the front of her dress. "A little late tonight, but I can make some calls in the morning."

"We'd appreciate that," Lola said, sliding from the stool. "What's his whole name anyway?"

Glenda smiled. "Now, dearie, if you was to know that, you wouldn't be tippin' me to make a phone call fer ya, would ya?"

Lola laughed. "You're right, luv. Call me at the club."

"I'll do it."

Outside and back in the cab, Carter asked her, "Think she's legit?"

"Oh, yeah. She knows how to reach him."

"Where to now?"

"Home," she said. "We've done all we can do tonight."

There was one club in Southwark, across the Thames from Blackfriars, that Lola and Carter hadn't hit. It was called the Fisherman, and Lola hadn't taken Carter there because one of her old lovers whom she now despised ran it.

As Carter handed Lola from the cab in Vauxhall and accepted her offer of a bit of breakfast, Gerhard Rouse emerged from the fog hovering by the river and entered the Fisherman.

Rouse was a big, slab-sided man, top-heavy with wide shoulders, thick arms, and a barrel chest. Under a two-day growth of beard, his tanned face was weatherbeaten. His chin jutted, as if daring someone to take a slug at him, and his nose was large and flanked by watery eyes. The eyes looked as though they were constantly staring along a gunsight, predatory like a vulture's.

He pushed through the noisy crush of people, his eyes darting over the tables along the wall in the dark side of the club. He spotted his man and pushed past the hanging symbols of the sea: fishnets, oars, anchors, and splintered mast poles.

"Nodo."

"Rouse."

Damon Nodoramus was a gangling, clean-shaven man with an ugly, pitted face who might be young or old. He was eating a fish that still had its head on, and was drinking lager in great gulps. The fish's eyes looked alive.

"How does it go?" Rouse asked after a tired, skinny waitress took his order for a pint.

"The van is ready, twin rear doors like you wanted. I nicked a Ford Escort about an hour ago. That's the one I'll roll."

Rouse nodded as the waitress brought his pint and wandered away. "And the pickup cars?"

"A Rover and a Cortina. The Rover's yours. You can drive it right to Heathrow and park it. I'll have it picked up after a couple of days."

Rouse lit a slender cigar and thought for a few moments, sipping his beer. "Our pigeon arrives at Heathrow tomorrow morning at six-ten. That means the Rover and the Cortina will have to be set tonight. I'll want to be on the M4 west of Paddington by six o'clock tomorrow morning. Any problem?"

Nodoramus shook his head. "We should meet at my brother's garage around five. You've got the hardware?"

"Two Stens. That's all we'll need."

The tall Greek shivered inside but he didn't let it show. This Rouse was a cold-blooded bugger. He didn't normally take a job where there was a "no witness" clause in the contract, but the money on this one was so good he couldn't refuse.

"What if the bloke misses the plane?"

"I've got that covered," Rouse replied. "I've also got a spotter at the airport to give us the car and the number. Anything else?"

"No. You're sure he'll go the M4?"

"I'm sure," Rouse said. "It's the only way he can get to Wales." His cold eyes narrowed. "You come recommended, Nodo. Don't let me down."

"I say I'll do a job, I do it."

"See that you do."

Rouse stood, dropped some bills on the table, and walked away.

Idly, he wondered if he should have mentioned to Nodo that he had been trailed across Europe, and that whoever that someone was, he was probably in England.

No, the less Nodo and Vrain knew, the better.

Carter lit a cigarette and sat back in his chair with a sigh. "I thought you couldn't cook."

Lola chuckled. "Anybody can boil water and fry eggs."

"It was delicious," he said, watching her dump the dishes in the sink with an economy of movement.

"You look as though you could bloody well fall asleep right there."

"I could," he replied. "I've only catnapped in the last forty-eight hours."

"You got a place?"

He nodded. "A company flat off Charing Cross."

"God, that's clear across town. It'll take you two hours in morning traffic."

"I know," he said, wearily heaving himself to his feet. "I'd better move."

Lola stopped him with a hand on the elbow as he passed toward his coat. "Carter . . ."

"Yeah?"

"I guess for six-fifty a day I can let ya crash on the couch. It's big enough."

"I wouldn't want to put you out," he replied dryly.

"Then piss off, ya bloody bugger."

"But if you'll throw in a shower, you've got a deal."

Carter stood, letting the warm water cascade over his body. It pounded over his face and drummed in his ears so he barely heard the shower door open.

He opened one eye. Lola stood in the opening, one foot on the edge of the tub. She was nude, and the sight of her breasts jutting their dark tips at him through the steam made him wonder just how tired he really was.

"Aren't you going to invite me in?"

"It's your shower."

She stepped into the shower and let her body slide against his under the water. The scent of her hair and perfume reached his nostrils. With her eyes closed, she felt for the soap dish, found the oval cake, and began moving it languidly over his chest.

"I thought you hated my guts."

"I do." The soap moved lower.

"I thought I was anathema."

"You are, but I got to remembering that afternoon on the Riviera."

"I didn't know I'd made such an impression. Is this part of the six-fifty as well?"

"Shut yer bloody face and scrub my back."

She pressed forward and kissed him. Purposefully, she clung to him, holding her arms tightly around his neck, rubbing her wet breasts hotly against his chest.

Carter rubbed back, his fingers doing a number on the small of her back and moving down.

He faced her head-on and pressed up against her. Her hands went between them, groped, and moved him between her thighs. Then she squeezed her legs together slightly to hold him there.

Carter's ears buzzed with the sound of the water and her heavy breathing in his ear. His hands lathered her body with the soap. Her breasts were rubbed and caressed until the nipples were standing up, rigidly erect. They pressed hotly into his chest.

"I want you," he rasped.

"Here? In the shower?"

"Why not?"

Then he suddenly picked up her soap-slick body. He held her under the armpits as she clasped her legs around his waist. Then he leaned her against the wall under the shower nozzle. The jets of stinging water cascaded down on them both.

He used one hand to guide his throbbing erection toward her. She clung to him and moaned as he slid into her easily.

He began to rotate, the water flowing warmly around the spot where they were joined together. He had increased the pressure and adjusted the nozzle so the stinging little bullets of water bounced on their skin.

In and out, in and out, he moved. Continuous moans of happiness bubbled from her lips as he moved with longer and harder strokes.

She groaned louder. As she opened her mouth the water spilled into it. She sputtered and choked, but nothing could mask the wonderful tingling in her body. It spread over her until she didn't think she'd be able to stand anymore.

Carter was beginning to pant. They clung together and wriggled in the luxurious soap and water that ran in rivers over their driving, thrusting bodies. He was pulsating. He felt his excitement rising to a peak. She lathered her hand and reached down between his legs.

That was all she had to do. Carter groaned long and loud.

They exploded together, their bodies writhing. She clung hard to his neck, shaking as the thrill, like an electric shock, rippled through her body.

Slowly, she lowered her feet back to the tub. "Lovely way to end the day."

They stepped from the shower and dried each other with huge, thick towels. Then she leaned her cheek against his neck and burrowed into his warmth. "You do have your moments, Carter."

Carter could feel himself beginning to slip off into a haze of weary contentment. He could feel her breath and the pattern of her soft body against him. "You mind too much if we go to bed now?"

"You sharing my bed?" she asked.

He nodded. "I checked the couch."

They moved from the steamy bathroom into her bedroom, lit dimly by one lamp. Still damp, Lola let herself fall onto the soft bed. Her arm flopped over his body as he joined her.

"Good night," she whispered.

Carter was already asleep.

THREE

Carter slipped from the bed, threw some water on his face, and dressed. Outside the window, it was another gray, winter day. It even looked colder than the day before, with a chance that the rain would turn to snow.

Lola was curled toward the center of the bed, her head buried in pillows. The covers had slipped off most of her beautiful behind.

He thought of writing a note, then decided that it would be safer to speak to her. The day's events were too important to leave anything to chance communications.

Gently he shook her shoulder. "Serena . . ."

"Unh."

"Lola, wake up."

"Go to hell."

"I'm going now."

"Good."

Carter smiled. The old Serena gleamed through like a bad penny. "I'll call in every half hour."

"You do that."

"Bless you," he said, and whacked her on the butt.

He could hear her curses all the way to the street. He

crossed the bridge and found a coffee shop. After wolfing down a breakfast, he grabbed a cab to the flat on Charing Cross Road. There, he shaved and climbed into fresh clothes.

The previous evening he'd waltzed around London unarmed. Today perhaps being D-Day, he slid Wilhelmina's rig over his shoulder and strapped Hugo's chamois sheath to his right forearm. The former was a 9mm Luger, the latter a razor-sharp, eight-inch stiletto.

The scramble line to AXE headquarters in the Amalgamated Press and Wire Services Building on Dupont Circle in Washington, D.C., was clear. He got through to David Hawk's office immediately. The call was picked up by the chief of AXE's right hand, Ginger Bateman.

"I'm hustling and I've got a little help," Carter said in response to her first query. "But so far, ziltch."

"Not much more here," the sable-haired beauty from Atlanta drawled. "We've run everything, governmental and military, through the computer, and nothing is happening in London or the rest of England for the next month."

"That doesn't mean he couldn't be here for something private."

"Sure," Bateman replied, "but that's impossible to check."

"Check anyway," Carter said. "Rouse is here for something. The Nodo character that he's contacted is a wheel man. Rouse is going to heist something."

"I'll do what I can. Stay in touch."

Carter hung up and cabbed to Scotland Yard. He had the blessings of some very high people in MI5 and 6, so there was no problem. He indexed, cross-indexed, and up-indexed every man and woman in the files who had ever driven for hire and been caught.

There wasn't a Nodo in the bunch.

Every hour, he called La Lola. "Any calls?"

"None yet, Nick."

"You were exciting last night."

"You were adequate," she said through a yawn. "How about lunch?"

"Stay by the phone."

At one o'clock, he broke for lunch and then walked across Whitehall to MI5. There he went through the same process with their terrorist files.

Still nothing.

On the Strand, he found a cozy pub, ordered a pint, and called Lola again.

"It's a bingo. Glenda called. Nodo moves around a lot, hard to get a line on."

"How well I know," Carter groaned. "What have you got?"

"Lately, he's been getting his equipment from a guy named Little, Harper Little. Runs a garage on Cable Street in Whitechapel."

"Lola, you're divine."

"You owe me thirteen hundred pounds."

"I'll pay you at dinner."

He looked up the address, paid for the beer, and hit the street. It took him a good ten minutes to get a cab.

"Where to, mate?"

"Whitechapel . . . Cable Street. What's with all the traffic?"

"BBC predicts snow. Everyone's gettin' home early."

It took nearly an hour to get clear across to the East End of London. Carter spotted the sign above the garage, and told the driver to go a little farther and park.

He dropped a twenty over the seat. "Wait, all right?"

"Sure, mate. Watch yerself around here."

"Oh?"

"Yeh. In this neighborhood they'll cut yer throat and piss

on the wound to stop the bleedin'."

"Thanks."

Carter retraced the two blocks on foot. It was a rickety old building at best, and in the gray gloom and rain it seemed sinister and isolated from reality.

The small, hand-lettered sign above the big pull-up door read, LITTLE'S—NO CREDIT. There was a smaller, duck-in door to the side. Carter pushed it open and walked inside.

There were two grease racks, occupied, and a center lane where three cars could be worked on at the same time. Beyond that, there was another big double door. Since the building was long and narrow, Carter assumed there was a second room to the garage.

To his left there was a ratty office, untidy and filthy. The desk was old and grubby, with bent handles on the drawers and bits of wood chipped off the corners. It was piled high with papers.

He was about to shuffle through the papers, when the door to the rear room slammed open and two men emerged. One was a giant in greasy blue coveralls, with more grease embedded forever in his face and the skin of his hands. The other was a short, gaunt man with slicked-back hair and a weasel face sporting a pencil-thin mustache. He wore a shoddy blue pin-striped suit, a red vest, and a gaudy, mismatched tie. He looked and spoke like a pimp.

"I been to his digs, Harp. He ain't been there fer days." From the slur in the smaller man's words he had obviously been drinking heavily.

"That ain't my problem, Jimmy."

The little man began to whine. "C'mon, Harp, I know you and Damon got a good popper goin'. Just a hunnert quid. He'll give it back to ya . . ."

"Can't do it, Jimmy. He told me . . ."

The two men had reached the office door. When the big

one saw Carter he stopped cold.

"Here we are. What can I do fer ya?"

"Harper Little?"

"That's me."

Carter threw a wary look from Little to the one called Jimmy and back again. "A lady told me I might find Nodo through you."

"Oh?"

His eyes went through Carter like an X-ray machine, and the Killmaster knew that the shoulder rig holding the Luger had been spotted. In the U.K. not many people walk around sporting guns in shoulder holsters. Those who do are usually the real good guys or the real bad guys.

"Yeah," Carter said. "I thought we might be able to do a wee bit of business together."

"What kind of business would that be?" the pimp asked.

Carter shrugged, his eyes on the big man. "I'm only in London for a few days. I might need a bit of chauffeuring . . ."

"Nodo, he's busy now—" Jimmy began, but was immediately interrupted by Little.

"Shut up, Jimmy, an' get yerself outta here."

"Gar, Harp, all I—"

"Shut up, I said. Now git!"

Jimmy glowered at both men and, shrinking in his suit, tottered to the door. When it slammed shut, Little turned back to Carter. "You look a little like a copper."

"I'm American."

"They got coppers in the colonies."

"Why don't you let Nodo decide? Can you get in touch with him?"

"Maybe I can, maybe I can't. You got a name . . . a number where I can reach ya?"

Carter jotted Lola's number on a pad, tore the page off,

and passed it over. "If a woman answers, she's okay. Tell Nodo I got to hear from him by tonight."

"An' if ya don't?"

Carter shrugged. "I'm paying damn good. There're other chauffeurs."

He left it at that and moved out of the office. The door to the rear room was still open and he cased it as he passed.

No repair going on there, and there was a marked difference between the shiny new vehicles in the rear room and the crates being worked on in the front. Something else was odd about them: no license plates.

Carter hit the street and headed toward the cab. Halfway there, he passed a narrow alley. Out of the corner of his eye he saw the pimp lounging near the mouth of the alley.

"Hey, mister . . ."

"Yeah?"

"Damon and I, we's in the same business."

"That so?" Carter started to walk on.

"Hey, wait up there. You ain't gonna get Damon to work no job now. I'm as good as he, you ask anybody."

"Sorry, mate, I can't use anybody who's been in the nick."

"I ain't never been nicked, I swear! I'm as clean as Damon!"

That, Carter thought, explained it. If Damon was Nodo, and Damon had no rap sheet, no wonder he hadn't been able to find him.

"You ever worked for Damon?"

"Hell, yes. He's me brother! We're thick, we are."

Carter tried not to look like he was jumping on it. He pulled out his pad and pen.

"Give me your name and a number where I can reach you."

Quickly, the little man scrawled on the pad and passed it back. "I can do ya good, I can. An' there's lotsa places I can get yer equipment besides Harp's . . . cheaper, too."

"We'll be in touch," Carter said, and moved on.

"Where to now?" the driver asked as Carter slid into the rear seat.

"Get about a mile away and find a pub with a phone."

"I don't mean to be nosy, mate, but are you a copper?"

"Kind of," Carter replied, and flipped the little notebook open.

The little pimp had scrawled a number and a name: Jimmy Nodoramus.

Five minutes later Carter stepped out of the cab in front of a neighborhood local called the Four Bells.

"Join me for a pint?"

"I really shouldn't."

Carter could tell that he really wanted to. "With the tip you're going to get, you can knock off the rest of the day."

The driver followed him inside. At the bar, they ordered two pints and Carter found the phone. It was in an ornate cage in the rear next to the rest rooms. He dropped a coin in the slot and dialed the digits for information.

"May I help you?"

"Yes, do you have a listing for Damon Nodoramus?"

"One moment, please." Carter lit a cigarette and drummed his fingers on the glass. "That's a Hounslow number, but I can't give it out. I'm afraid it's unlisted."

"This is police business."

"I'm sorry, sir . . ."

Carter hung up and fished another coin from his pocket.

A gruff voice answered on the first ring. "Scotland Yard."

"Bronson Wyckoff, please."

"Who's calling?"

"Nick Carter."

"A moment."

It was more like three before Wyckoff came on with his Scottish burr. "Nick, lad, heard you were in town and pokin' our computers. Sorry I missed ya!"

"I've been a little busy, Bronson. I need a favor."

"See what I can do."

"Damon Nodoramus. He's got an unlisted number in Hounslow. I need an address."

"Take about twenty minutes."

"I'm in a pub." Carter gave him the number and hung up.

At the bar, he jawed with the cab driver and a couple of oldsters. The main topics were the price of gasoline, the Common Market, and Fergie the Fantastic.

"Call fer a Nick?"

"That's me. Thanks, mate." Carter hurried to the cage and waited until the barman hung up before he spoke. "I'm on."

"Twenty-four Pekin Mews. That's about three miles this side of Heathrow. You need directions?"

"I've got a cab. Thanks, Brons."

"Good enough, Nick. Ring me before ya leave, we'll bend an elbow."

"I'll do that."

Carter dropped a fiver on the bar and upended his pint.

"We go?"

"We go," Carter said.

Pekin Mews was a cul-de-sac of row houses, old and weathered. Each of them had one flat up and one down. Number Twenty-four was up, reached through a covered stairwell.

Carter got no answer to his ring, and the vestibule door was locked. Shielding with his body, he called on American Express and opened the spring lock. One the top floor he used his picks to get into the flat proper.

Gray light from dirty windows filtered over shiny, tasteless furniture of the kind that comes with medium-range apartments and tells nothing about the occupant. The living room was large, there was a full kitchen, a dining room, and a single bedroom with a tiny bath.

The whole flat was meticulously clean, as opposed to the outside of the windows. Unlike the furniture, a row of about a dozen suits in the bedroom closet were very expensive. They were all handmade, and would run a good two hundred pounds in some upscale shop on Regent Street. The shirts and ties were the same.

Whatever Damon Nodoramus did, he made a good piece of change at it.

The desk was as neat as the closet. He found receipts, canceled checks, and finally a checkbook. The balance was healthy and the deposits, far apart, were large. The contents of a file drawer told him why.

Damon Nodoramus was a race car driver. For the past two years he had made an above-average income testing new tire models for all the big tire manufacturers. It also appeared as though he represented a couple of small auto parts manufacturers.

The bottom drawer on the right side was locked. It took two picks and some sweat, but Carter finally got it open.

Wrapped in tissue and held together with a rubber band, he found a packet of pornographic pictures. They were all of the same man and the same woman, and they all looked homemade. In the bottom of the drawer was a tin box, also locked.

Carter set it on top of the desk, picked it, and whistled.

Inside were stacks of five-hundred-pound notes. A quick count told Carter that he was looking at nearly a quarter of a million. Nodo's moonlighting business paid a lot better than his regular work.

Shoved in among the bills was a slip of paper:

Rover	£2200
Cortina	£1850
Harp	£3000

Collect from R. £7050 over contract

Carter smiled. Nodo was indeed a meticulous man.

He closed his eyes and concentrated until the rear room of Little's Garage became clear in his mind. He saw a gray van, a blue Ford Escort, a Rover four-door, and a Cortina.

Quickly, he relocked the box, put it back in the drawer and locked it.

In the living room he found the phone on a small table with an ashtray from Penny's, Surrey, and a Rolodex. In the bottom of the ashtray was a logo of a naked female.

Carter took the phone apart to make sure it wasn't bugged, reassembled it, and dialed from memory.

"One-five-five," said a machine. "You have reached Special Branch. State your name, your business, and the number you are calling from. Your call will be returned at once."

He waited for the beep and spoke. "Carter, N3, Washington. My business is with Claude Dakin. Hounslow 7791."

He hung up and reached for the pack of cigarettes in his pocket, then thought better of it. The single ashtray in the flat didn't necessarily mean that Nodo smoked. If he didn't, he would have a sensitive nose and know that someone had been in his digs.

Impatiently Carter paced the room waiting for the phone to ring. Twice he passed the mantel before his eye fell on a framed photo, and locked.

She was Chinese, slim and young, with good legs and an excellent figure. Her makeup was overdone . . . pale lipstick, green eye shadow, and carefully lacquered hair. The overall effect was theatrical, eye-catching.

She wore a Chinese *cheongsam,* snugly fitted, high-collared, short-sleeved, with the skirt split to where her panties would normally be. She wore none.

The inscription read: *Damon, my love, may we always enjoy your hobby together. Your Lin.*

It wasn't hard to figure out Damon's "hobby." Lin was the girl in the porno photos in the man's desk. Carter didn't have a description of Nodo, but he guessed that he was the other star in the photos.

Carter went through the Rolodex quickly. There was no Lin, and no Chinese last name.

He grabbed the phone on the first ring, but didn't speak.

"Hello? Hello? Nick?"

"Hello, Claude. Sorry, I'm in a place where I shouldn't be . . . I wanted to be sure it was you. I need a favor."

"What's the problem"

"That's just it," Carter replied, "I don't know. I need a couple of surveillance teams."

There was a groan on the other end of the line. "We're stretched, Nick, and I'm afraid every other agency is as well. I've even had to bring people in off holiday."

"What's up?"

"It's hush-hush, but I suppose I can tell you. Four muckety-mucks are flying into Heathrow tonight from OPEC. They have a conference with the P.M. It's only going to be four or five hours and they fly on to Paris. But we've had threats, the usual."

Carter's mind spun like a top. OPEC ministers? It didn't sound like Rouse's style. But he had to tell Dakin.

"I don't know, Nick, sounds like a long shot," the man replied when Carter had finished his tale. "But I'll tell you what. I'll put a team on this garage this afternoon. It's better to be safe than sorry."

"Thanks, Claude."

Carter hung up. He took a last look to make sure the apartment was as he'd found it, and split.

"Where to now, guy?"

Carter gave the cabbie the Charing Cross address, and leaned back in the seat.

More and more, the pursuit of Rouse looked like either a wild-goose chase or a crime in the making. And if Rouse was just flexing his muscles with an armored car or bankroll heist to keep his hand in, it was none of Carter's affair.

FOUR

British Airways flight 716's departure was announced over the loudspeaker system at Los Angeles International Airport. Passengers could now board if they wished, once electronically inspected and passed on into the clearance area.

A man listened to the announcement, finished the last of his beer, and ordered another one. Flight 716 was his flight, but he wasn't in a hurry. He made this flight once a month, and he always liked to be one of the last to board.

He looked slightly out of place among the pin-striped banker types around him at the bar. His light brown hair was a trifle long, curling over his ears and collar. His narrow, lean face was accented by a well-trimmed beard and mustache, the latter barely covering his upper lip. He wore a safari suit, the jacket belted, the pants flared. Mahogany zippered boots covered his feet.

He looked more like a well-heeled hippie than a businessman, but that was part of his image. When people asked him what he did, he always replied he was an agent who handled rock stars.

The image fit the name: Ian Pierce.

Actually, Ian Pierce was chief courier for Brandeis Limited. Brandeis was a jointly owned British and American aerospace company with offices in Los Angeles, California, and Cardiff, South Wales. Their testing laboratories and think tanks were located in the midland area of Wales, where, at one time, the only industry was coal mining.

Brandeis was a specialized company and very unique. While Lockheed, Martin-Marietta, and myriad other companies created space-age arms and their components, Brandeis tested them and passed their results on to the Pentagon and Whitehall.

Few people even knew of the company's existence, let alone its reason for being. And that was the way its executive officers wanted it. Brandeis didn't even use telex or any means of satellite communications. When specifications and plans were passed from office to office, or office to testing facility, it was done by courier, hand to hand.

Pierce finished his second beer, paid the bartender, and hoisted his calfskin bag. It was a unique bag because it combined a small, carry-on section for the barest necessities, and a briefcase in its center section.

He went through security easily because the only metal he carried was a gold cigarette lighter. Pierce didn't smoke, but he always carried the cigarette lighter. Like the bag, it was unique. Properly used, it could spout a flesh-melting flame four inches wide and effective up to seven feet. It was an effective weapon, but Ian Pierce had never had to use it.

He walked down the long corridor to the departure gate for BA #716. A uniformed man glanced at his ticket, stamped it, and handed it back to him with his boarding pass and seat number.

"Have a nice flight, Mr. Pierce."

"Thank you."

A stewardess stood in the doorway and took his ticket again.

"Seven-D, Mr. Pierce. First-class section is just to your left." Her accent was decidedly French, but her body and chestnut hair and her hazel eyes were just nice in any language.

Pierce smiled at her and said in flawless French, "Thank you. What is a beautiful Parisian doing on a British Airways flight?"

"Ah, you speak French?" she asked, smiling.

"Of course, why shouldn't I"—he glanced at her name tag—"Christine?"

"You are American . . ."

"You are French, and you speak English."

Another passenger fidgeted behind Pierce. He winked at the pretty stewardess, mouthed "Later" with his lips, and moved on to his seat.

It took almost an hour for the plane to get off the ground because of the backup on the runways. It would taxi for a few yards, then stop. The pilot would rev the engines to an earsplitting whine, then decelerate, and the plane would hump forward another few yards. Pierce wished he could walk around instead of just sitting. The sign was implacable: *Fasten seat belts, no smoking.* Suppose a guy got the runs or had to puke? he wondered.

With all its perks, Ian Pierce loved his job, but he hated airplanes.

Finally the plane lifted off, and a sigh of relief could be sensed rather than heard throughout the cabin. A few moments later, the sign went off and the air grew thick with cigarette smoke.

Besides airplanes, Pierce hated cigarettes. He tried to ignore the smell, and leaned back in his seat, staring absently out the window at the gathering night.

The pretty stewardess came up the aisle and stopped at his seat.

"A drink, Monsieur Pierce?"

"*Une bière, s'il vous plaît.*"

"*Mais certainement.*"

When she returned with the drink she had in tow a short, heavyset man with a fringe of neatly trimmed gray hair around an otherwise bald head.

The stewardess served Pierce his beer and stepped out of the way. "I hope this seat will be more to your liking, Mr. Smythe."

"Jolly good. Thank you, dear." He settled into the seat and turned to Pierce. "Hope you don't mind, old man. Gave me a smoking-section ticket and I can't abide the foul habit."

Pierce shrugged, managed a smile, and turned back to the window. Within minutes his hopes for a quiet, uninterrupted journey were dashed.

"Travis Smythe," the man said, extending his hand.

"Ian Pierce," Pierce replied, shaking the offered hand.

Pierce noticed that the man's gray suit was of the first quality without being ostentatious, and he wore a subdued blue and black Royal Thames tie.

The man unfolded a copy of *The Economist* with a snap, but made no effort to read it. "Bank of England, myself. You?"

Pierce sighed. "I'm in show business, music."

"Music, eh? Good show. Remember years ago my wife used to yearn for the stage a bit. Thought she had a great voice, but no one else did." He laughed and Pierce turned back to the window. "She's dead now."

Pierce sighed inwardly, wanting to be alone with his

thoughts. He replied unenthusiastically. "Sorry."

"Quite all right. The old girl was years older than I, actually. Had a good life."

"Excuse me." Pierce leaned toward the window and feigned sleep.

God, he thought, *all I need all the way to London is a jolly chap from the old boys' club!*

Carter ground out his cigarette in the back of the cab and checked his watch. It was two in the morning. They had been parked in Hounslow since ten, directly across from Damon Nodoramus's flat.

The man had never shown, and no one else had entered or left the flat.

The driver snored smoothly in the front seat. Carter eased out of the cab and walked a half block to a phone booth.

"Hello?"

"Sab . . . ."

"Lola."

"All right, Lola, it's me. Any calls?"

"None, nil, *nada*. What do I get for playing answering service?"

"My beautiful body," Carter growled.

There was a short pause and then a laugh. "I'll take it."

Carter hung up and returned to the cab. He woke up the driver and gave him the Charing Cross address. Around Marble Arch, he changed his mind.

In front of Lola's nightclub, he paid the cabbie off for the day and included a fat tip.

"Many thanks, guv. Here's me card if ya need me again."

Carter saluted him and entered the club. Lola was holding court behind the bar. When she spotted him, she came over.

"You just got a call a couple of minutes ago."

"Yeah?"

"Gent named Claude. He said you know the number."

"Yeah, I do."

Carter used the pay phone and got right through to Claude Dakin.

"Nick, no action at your garage. I had to pull my people off to cover the hotel at the airport. Sorry."

"That's okay, Claude," Carter replied. "I think I may be tilting at windmills anyway."

He hung up and went back to the bar. Lola had a tall one waiting for him.

"How we doin'?"

"We're not," he replied, sipping the drink.

"You leavin'?"

He shook his head. "Not for a couple of days. Got to see whatever it is through."

"Good," she said. "I'm actually beginning to enjoy yer miserable company." She dropped the key to her upstairs apartment on the bar.

After dinner, Ian Pierce slept through the movie, more to avoid his seatmate's chattering than anything else. When he awoke they were about an hour out of Heathrow and the cabin crew was serving juices, rolls, and coffee.

Travis Smythe wasn't in his seat.

Pierce grabbed his bag and went aft to the washroom. Just as he was about to enter, he saw Smythe at the other end of the walk-through having a smoke and watching the sun come up. Pierce darted quickly inside to avoid the man.

He locked the door and used the toilet facilities. He washed his hands, went over his face quickly with a battery-razor, and splashed on some after shave.

He just hit his seat again when Christine brought a tray.

"Sorry about that," she said.

"What's that?"

"The bore I put beside you. But he insisted on a non-smoking seat, and you had the only one."

"Nonsmoking . . ."

She nodded. "Said they gave him a smoking-section seat by mistake. Excuse me."

She hurried off to answer a call, and Pierce sipped his coffee. Nonsmoking, he thought, watching the gray dawn wheel slowly through the porthole and pick up motes of dust suspended in the air. If Smythe was a nonsmoker, why had he gone aft to cadge a cigarette in the smoking section?

He had just about decided that perhaps the man was trying to quit, when the engines, barely noticeable in their constant tone, dropped an octave.

The background tinkle of music stopped and a confident voice said, "Good morning, ladies and gentlemen. This is Captain Johns speaking. We are at present descending from thirty-four thousand feet and expect to be landing in twenty-three minutes. Surface temperature is five degrees Celsius under mostly cloudy skies."

The smooth baritone continued, "Please fasten your seat belts and observe the No Smoking signs. We hope that you have enjoyed your flight with British Airways as much as we have enjoyed having you with us." The Muzak resumed and the seat-belt sign winked on.

"Looks like typically beastly weather, doesn't it?" Smythe said, lowering himself into his seat.

Ian Pierce shrugged. "England."

Liam Vrain, a stoop-shouldered little man in a rain slicker with a tweed cap pulled low over his beady eyes, stared myopically through the slashing wipers.

"Bloody rain."

"Be glad it isn't snow," Rouse said from the other seat.

"Bloody rain," Vrain said again, as if he hadn't heard the other man.

The gray van traveled at an even sixty-five, headlights showing a desolate nothing on either side of the motorway.

"There's the cutout," Rouse said. "Turn off."

Vrain wheeled the van to the left and checked the rearview mirror. Damon Nodoramus was right behind them in the Escort.

"Pull up right beside the telephone box."

Vrain braked and the Escort pulled up alongside them.

"What now?" Vrain asked.

"We wait for the call."

The big plane taxied to the terminal after an uneasy three-bump landing. Passengers, including Smythe, began pulling their luggage down from the overheads and crowding the aisles long before the plane came to a stop.

Ian Pierce didn't move.

The plane's public address system came on to announce that British Airways hoped its passengers had enjoyed their journey and would give the airline the further pleasure of serving them again soon.

The doors opened and the crowd began to move. Ian Pierce was in no hurry. He waited until nearly all the passengers were off, and then joined the line.

Passport and customs were routine. Smythe wasn't in sight. Pierce got through and headed for the taxi stand. He was fifth in line. Slowly he inched toward the starter.

"Where to, sir?"

"Piccadilly Hotel, please."

A cab pulled up and Pierce got in. "Piccadilly Hotel," said the starter, and the driver pulled away.

Just outside the gate, Pierce leaned forward and dropped a twenty-pound note onto the seat beside the driver. "I've changed my mind. Pull into parking lot Two, there."

"The car park? But the starter said . . ."

Pierce smiled. "I just remembered someone was meeting me. You can make twenty quid, get right back in line, and make another twenty."

The driver shrugged. "Up to you, mate."

He pulled into the vast parking lot, rolled by six of the aisles, and Pierce called a halt.

"Have a nice day," Pierce chuckled, and stepped out of the cab.

When the cab rounded a lane and disappeared, Pierce moved through the cars of row 14A until he came to a new Jaguar four-door. Inside were two men, one reading the morning *Times*, the other penciling in the crossword.

Pierce tapped on the window and the two men came alive. Lyman Harris, a big, spare man in his mid-thirties, conservatively dressed, with his sandy hair trimmed in a brush cut, jumped from the passenger seat and opened the rear door.

"Good morning, Mr. Pierce. Good flight?"

"The usual, tiring," Pierce said, sliding into the rear seat. "Morning, Roddy, how's the new baby?"

Rodney McCay, also large and beefy, was in his twenties and always smiling. "Toddlin' already, sir."

The door closed behind Lyman Harris and the big car was moving.

"If you both don't mind," Pierce said, "I'm just going to stretch out."

"You do that, Mr. Pierce," McCay said. "Get yerself some rest and we'll have you in Cardiff safe and sound when ya wake up."

• • •

On the outdoor observation deck on the roof of the terminal, Travis Smythe watched the dark blue Jaguar leave the parking lot through powerful binoculars. Beneath them, his lips moved as he recited the license plate numbers over and over to himself.

When he had them embedded in his mind and the car had reached the main exit road out of Heathrow, he stowed the glasses back in his bag and went back into the terminal. At a news kiosk on the main concourse, he changed three one-pound notes and found a bank of phones. From under his watchband he withdrew a small slip of paper and dialed a number.

The phone rang twice and was picked up. "Yes."

"Dark blue Jaguar, four-door. Two men in the front, both armed. He is in the back seat."

"Number?"

"U.K. plate DDH four-fiveIE. It also has a large aerial on the boot lid."

"How long ago?"

"Less than five minutes."

"Gents, across from Pan Am counter. Second booth to your right. It's taped under the tank." The line went dead.

Travis Smythe followed the overhead signs to the Pan Am concourse, and found the men's washroom. Inside, he stooped to make sure the second booth was empty, and opened the door.

Taped to the bottom of the tank was a key. On it was stamped Blue 24.

Back on the concourse, he found three sets of luggage lockers, one yellow, one green, and one blue. He opened number 24. Inside was a single, sealed white envelope.

He moved close to the locker, shielding the envelope with his body, and tore it open. Inside, he found an untraceable bearer bond worth ten thousand Swiss francs, and five thousand pounds in large denomination bills.

He smiled.

Travis Smythe didn't know his employer. In fact, he hadn't heard from the man for nearly three years, until he received the call two weeks earlier. But he certainly wished he were more active.

The assignments were always so easy, and so profitable.

He pocketed the bearer bond and the money, and crossed to the Pan Am ticket counter. "Good morning."

"Good morning, sir."

"I believe I have reservations on your eight-ten flight to Frankfurt."

"The name, sir?"

"Smythe, Travis Smythe," he said, and thought, *for now*.

"Yes. Mr. Smythe, I have it right here. Will that be cash or credit card?"

"Oh, cash," Smythe replied with a smile. "Definitely cash."

Gerhard Rouse hung up the phone and walked back to the Escort. Nodo rolled down the window and looked up at him through watery eyes.

"Bloody heater doesn't work."

Rouse's lips split in what, for him, was a smile. "Yer fault, Nodo. Check the iron out before you nick it for a job. He's in."

"Good-o. What's he look like?"

"Four-door, dark blue Jag. Tag is DDH forty-fiveIE. My man says it's got an aerial on the rear, a big one, probably a two-way outfit."

Nodo nodded. "Be easy to spot. How many?"

"Two in front, like always. Our boy's in the back. Call me on yer walkie when you make 'em."

"I'll do it."

Rouse walked back to the van and climbed into the passenger seat. "Let's go. Nodo will double back and let us know when they pass him."

"Right," Vrain replied, putting the van into gear and moving out of the cutout. "Bloody snow."

Rouse jerked his head up. The rain had indeed turned to snow, and it looked heavy.

FIVE

Pierce mumbled awake and sat up in the rear seat as the Jaguar started over the Severn Bridge.

"Where are we?"

"Just past Bristol on the M4. We'll be through Newport in about ten minutes. The Risca cutoff is just beyond."

"About another hour then?" Pierce said.

"Something like that, sir. There's a little place in the hills just before Risca. Would you fancy some lunch?"

"No," Pierce replied, "not until I've made my delivery. Say, can you turn the heat up a little back here?"

"Sure thing, sir."

McCay cranked the heater fan up, and minutes later they dropped off the M4 onto a narrow, winding road north toward the village of Risca and the main offices of Brandeis Limited.

They drove at a steady pace for about three miles in silence. The snow was coming down in thick, soggy flakes now, but it was starting to stick. The hilly landscape where miners had once worked twenty-four hours a day taking out coal was turning from brown to white.

"Bloody fool," McCay suddenly hissed, and dropped

the powerful car into third gear for a curve.

"What is it?" Harris asked.

"Little Ford behind us, bugger's in a hell of a hurry." McCay got around the curve, slowed, and edged as far to the left as he could. "All right, you bloody maniac, go on around!"

The smaller car spurted abreast of them, its engine whining and its back wheels spinning so much that its rear end was fishtailing.

Harris chuckled from the passenger seat. "Probably trying to make opening time at the Crown in Risca."

"If ya ask me," McCay replied, "the bloody fools's had a few already."

The little car darted in front of them, fishtailed a time or two more, and found some traction. About two hundred yards ahead there was a wide S-curve.

"He'd better slow down," Pierce said from the rear seat, "or he'll never make the second part of that curve."

"Serve the bugger right," McCay rasped.

The words were scarcely out of his mouth when the tail end of the Escort swung out to the right. The driver fought the wheel but his speed was too great to arrest the spin when the tail came back to the left.

His left rear fender clipped a tree as the little car slid off the road. The impact spun him the other way and the driver lost it.

"Damn!" Harris cried out. "He's goin' over!"

Both wheels on the right side had gotten just enough bite at the top of the spin to launch the car into the air. The occupants of the Jaguar saw the underside of the smaller car, and then the Escort was on its roof. The top caved in and held as the car spun like a top. As the revolutions ceased, the Escort flipped over onto its passenger side and came to rest.

"Bloke'll be lucky his neck ain't broke. I'll have a look."

McCay slid the Jaguar to a halt and Harris popped out the passenger side. As Harris moved toward the Escort, McCay opened his own door and stood, one foot on the ground and one leg still in the car.

Behind them, a gray van rounded the first part of the S-curve and slowed.

Harris was about ten yards from the up-ended Escort when the door lifted in the air and the driver stood up in the opening.

Ian Pierce didn't see him. He had glanced through the rear window of the Jaguar to see one of the van's occupants jump to the ground. As the man ran toward the Jaguar through the snow, he lifted his arms. It was a second or two before Pierce saw the Sten gun.

"McCay . . ."

But Rodney McCay had troubles of his own. A Sten gun had appeared in the Escort driver's hands. McCay was clawing under his coat for his service revolver, but he was too late.

The Sten gun opened up and steel-jacketed slugs tore into Harris. The body spun, doing a grotesque dance, and fell into the snow.

At the same time, the rear window of the Jaguar blew up. McCay whirled, saw the danger, and ran to the rear of the car. He dropped to one knee and got off a single shot at the running figure before a burst from the Sten tore into his chest.

Ian Pierce opened the rear door and rolled into the snow. The Jaguar was in a withering cross fire now. The driver of the Escort and the man from the van were running full tilt, their weapons on automatic.

Pierce moved forward. He saw an irregular line of jagged holes along the side of the Jaguar's hood. Some of the bullets had ripped long, ragged grooves across it.

Suddenly there was a lull in front of the car. Pierce poked his head around the fender. The man was jamming a fresh clip into his Sten.

"Nodo, he's coming for you!"

Pierce took off at a dead run. He fumbled the gold lighter from his pocket and adjusted it by feel.

Damon Nodoramus was bringing his Sten up to fire, when a sheet of flame burst from his target. It engulfed him from head to toe. He screamed in agony and flung the Sten away as he fell to the snow and writhed in pain.

Pierce ran by the screaming man and dived for the protection of the upturned car.

He never made it.

Gerhard Rouse aimed two feet in front of Pierce and sprayed backward. Three slugs entered Pierce's brain and ten others stitched along his body.

He was dead when he hit the snow.

Vrain joined Rouse, and together they ran to kneel by Nodo.

"Jesus," the little man in the rain slicker gasped, and turned aside to retch in the snow.

The snow had extinguished the fire burning Nodo's clothes, but they still smoldered. Where the clothes had been burned away, the flesh beneath them was charred black and already peeling off in strips. One side of his face was gone, and where his right eye had been there was only a hole in his skull. His left eye still had sight, and it glared up at Rouse as the half of his mouth left screamed in agony.

"Get him in the van," Rouse growled.

"Gawd, oh Gawd," Vrain choked, and retched again.

Rouse slung his Sten, grabbed Vrain by his hair, and turned him around. He slapped him, open-handed, back and forth, until the man's gibberish stopped.

"Get him in the fucking van and be quick about it!"

Averting his eyes, Vrain grabbed Nodo by the ankles and began dragging him through the snow toward the van.

Rouse checked all three men to make sure they were dead, and then trotted back to the Jaguar. He yanked Pierce's bag from the rear and moved on to the van. Vrain was just hoisting Nodo into the rear. By this time the man had passed out.

"Gawd, he's bad, real bad."

"Drive!" Rouse barked. "I'll see to him." He slammed the two rear doors and knelt by Nodo as the van was wheeled around in the road.

He checked the man's burns, his pulse, and rolled up his one good eye. The pupil had disappeared into his head.

"We gotta get him to hospital!" Vrain rasped.

"I don't think so."

"Huh?"

"He ain't gonna last an hour," Rouse said, and crawled into the front.

Back across the Severn Bridge, Vrain turned off the M4 onto a narrow road that eventually led north to Chipping Sodbury. Five miles farther on and still three miles short of the village, he wheeled off into a lane.

Minutes later, the lane widened and ended in a clearing. In the center of the clearing was a shed, its warping boards peeling paint and what roof was left about to cave in.

Behind the shed sat the Rover and the Ford Cortina.

Vrain had scarcely halted the van before Rouse was out his side and, Pierce's bag in one hand, jogging toward the Rover. He was tossing the bag into the rear when Vrain reached him.

"Here now, ya ain't just gonna leave Nodo to die, are ya?"

"He's already as good as dead," Rouse replied, jerking open the driver's side door of the Rover.

"Well, what about me money? If Nodo dies, how do I get the rest of me money?"

"You're right," Rouse said almost gently.

He raised the Sten and fired into Vrain's temple just below the hairline. The sound of the single shot was a sharp crack in the stillness.

It was just enough sound to rouse Nodo from his deathlike state. He raised himself on one elbow from the floor of the van. The movement almost brought another scream from his lips, but what he saw through the windshield stifled it.

It was half of Vrain's head spraying through the air and the man's body whirling and falling. Almost immediately, the snow around him turned crimson with his still-pumping blood.

"You bastard, Rouse, you dirty bastard."

He saw the stocky man slide into the Rover and heard the engine growl to life. Seconds later the car whirled around the van and was gone.

It took Nodo nearly an hour to crawl from the van to the Cortina. Twice he passed out. Only hatred for Rouse kept him going until he was upright in the driver's seat. But he was determined to survive.

If he lived through the next two or three hours, he was pretty sure he could pay the bastard back.

SIX

The phone rang and Carter opened his eyes to the clock.

Nine-thirty!

He had slept the sleep of the dead after finally nodding off about dawn.

The phone rang again with a nagging insistence, and he nudged the body beside him with an elbow.

"Are you awake?"

"No."

"Your phone is ringing."

"Who cares."

He reached over the valleys and hillocks of the somnolent body for the phone, and grumped into it. "Yes."

"Carter?"

He was instantly awake. "Yes, Claude."

"This was one of the two numbers you gave me. I tried—"

"Yes, Claude, what is it?"

"Bit of a mess in Wales this morning. Some of the pieces might fit in with this Little's Garage item you passed me yesterday."

"How so?" Carter asked, shaking a cigarette from his pack.

"It's a security item. That's why we were notified this morning. Three bodies. One of them was a courier for Brandeis Limited. You know about them?"

"No."

"I'll tell you on the way. I'm taking a helicopter from the St. James's pad. Can you make it in a half hour?"

"I'll be there."

Carter hung up and reached for his pants.

He glanced at Lola, exquisitely naked and totally uncovered, and shook his head. It had come down while he was romping in the sack, while he should have been on the streets. Guilt hit him like a shot of novocaine, numbing him.

"What's the matter?" she asked sleepily.

"I need your car."

She sat up, rubbing sleep from her eyes. "What's all the hurry up about?"

"Just give me your damn keys."

"All right, all right. My purse."

He tossed her the purse and finished dressing. By the time he was ready to go, she had found the keys and dropped them on the bed.

He paused going out the door. "It may or may not have anything to do with this Nodo, but they found three bodies in Wales this morning."

Before she could ask anything more, Carter was down the stairs.

Gerhard Rouse parked the Rover in lot Three at Gatwick Airport. Taking the bag, he walked to lot Two and unlocked the door of a Mini. It took a bit of a struggle, but he managed to get his bulk into the driver's seat.

If there was any kind of a leak and they found the Rover, the natural assumpiton would be that he had caught a plane out of the country.

Minutes later, he was on Route 23 heading south for Brighton. At Crawley, he turned off just long enough to make a phone call.

René Charmont sat in his sumptuous office, flicking his eye from the ornate clock on the wall to the Rhône. The river curved here, flowing like the smooth hip of a reclining woman around the five acres of the Charmont estate.

When the clock struck the hour, Charmont slammed the desk with the flat of his hand, stood, and began to pace the room.

Charmont was tall, very tall. Most people, when they first met him, found him unattractive. But after a short time their opinion, especially those of women, changed.

He had no pretensions to conventional good looks. He was too thin for his unusual height, although he compensated with a lithe, loose-limbed grace. It was the sort of body on which expensive hand-tailored clothes hung well, lending an unmistakable elegance to his natural grace. His hair, a sun-shot shade of blond, was fine and fell across one side of his high forehead. The planes of his face were sharply defined, the cheekbones dominating slightly gaunt cheeks. His nose was large and thin, yet aristocratically straight. The lines running from it to the edges of his mouth were deeply incised, indicating his life had not been easy.

That mouth was broad, perhaps too narrow, and his smiles tended to be crooked. But it was an expressive mouth, one that some might call sensual. Or cruel? His eyes were deep-set, with a disconcerting tendency to squint when he concentrated, emphasizing the network of lines at their corners. They were a clear, light blue, striking against his high, ruddy complexion.

Actually, his total appearance was slightly sinister. It fit the man.

He was about to press the intercom on his desk, when it buzzed. "Yes, Solange?"

"Your call from England, line two."

"*Merci, chérie.*" Charmont punched the button and grabbed the phone. "Yes?"

"It is done."

"Were there any problems?"

"None. The two Englishmen won't carry tales. I have the bag."

"And you're sure you are clear?" Charmont asked.

"Absolutely. I am on my way to Brighton now."

"Good. My people will meet you at the caravan tomorrow evening at eight sharp. And, Gerhard . . ."

"Yes?"

"A job well done. There will be a bonus, a substantial bonus."

"Right."

Charmont hung up and pushed the intercom button. "Solange, can you come up, please?"

Charmont lit a thin cigar. It was going well when his secretary, mistress, confidante, and chief executioner stepped into the room. Through the gray smoke he watched her approach, and smiled.

Solange Sasz was a tall woman, gorgeous. She was somewhere around thirty, but she hadn't aged a day in fifteen years, since René Charmont had plucked her from the gutters of Marseilles.

She wore a pair of tight slacks that emphasized her long, tapering legs and firm hips, and a silk blouse. Her hair was a thick auburn, and she had perfect features with perhaps slightly overlarge lips. They didn't detract from her beauty but merely added a touch of sensuousness to her already great sex appeal. Under the peasant-style blouse, her full breasts bobbled lazily, unfettered, making Charmont sigh.

Fifteen years, he thought, *and she excites me as much as she did the first day I met her.*

"Solange, take the helicopter. There is a four-fifteen flight from Nice directly into Gatwick."

"Rouse?"

"Yes, it went well. You have directions to the caravan?"

"Of course."

"Do it neatly, Solange. Leave no traces of yourself."

"Don't I always?"

Carter and Claude Dakin stayed out of the local constable's way. It didn't take more than a half hour to piece together what must have happened.

It was a slaughter. None of them had a chance. They did discover the lighter, and finally figured out how it was used.

"One of them," Dakin said, "got singed pretty badly."

"Anything on the Escort?"

Dakin nodded. "The locals just got word from the Yard. It was nicked in London night before last, an underground garage in the City. Belonged to a young accountant working late. You think it was the same Escort you saw in the back of Little's Garage?"

Carter shrugged. "Impossible to say."

"Well, I've had the Yard pick up Harper Little, but I doubt if we'll get much out of him."

A late-model Saab pulled up to the barricades, and a tall, stern-faced man got out. He conversed briefly with the uniformed constable, who pointed to Carter and Dakin. The tall man nodded and hurried their way.

"Mr. Dakin? Mr. Carter?" They both nodded. "Paul Hughes. I'm head of security for Brandies. I just got the clearance from California to give you details and cooperate any way I can."

"How grand," Dakin said dryly. "Why don't we use

one of the cars? It's warmer."

They were just settled in when the chief constable, a ruddy-faced man with a walrus mustache, tapped on the window.

"Mr. Dakin, sir, another body has just been found, across the Severn near Chipping Sodbury."

"Oh, right, I seen this big Rover go by me like a bloomin' bullet, I did. I was over there right behind that hedgerow, I was, gonna get me a couple of birds fer supper, I was. They comes out so's you can see 'em easy in snow like this, ya know."

"Yes," Dakin nodded, and glanced at Carter.

"And then what happened?" the Killmaster asked.

The big farmer scratched his stubble for a few seconds, shifted his shotgun to his other shoulder, and pointed.

"Come from there, I did. I decided to change me spot. There were about a half hour or so after I spotted the Rover go by. I walks in here and the first thing I sees is that bloke there with the hole in his head."

Dakin moved to a patch of blood in the snow, and pointed down. "And this was where you saw the burned man?"

"Aye. He was lyin' there dead, he was. Leastways, he sure looked dead to me."

"Obviously," Carter said, "he was alive."

"I s'pose he was. I mean, he musta been, to have drove off whilst I ran to me house and called the coppers."

"And you're sure that it was a Cortina parked there behind the shed?"

"As sure as I'm here. Me boy just got one near like it."

Carter's eyes followed the bloody path in the snow the where the Cortina had been parked. From the farmer's description of the man, he had to be close to death. Yet he had managed to drag himself to the car and drive away.

"Claude . . ."

The Special Branch man left the farmer in the hands of the chief constable, and followed Carter as he walked back to the van.

"Not much doubt now, is there?"

The Killmaster shook his head. "The four vehicles are the same ones I saw in the back of the Little's Garage. But, as you said, it will be hell getting him to talk. The one thing we've got going for us is Damon Nodoramus. Rouse probably doesn't know that we've got a name."

"What's our best shot?"

"You get back to London and Nodoramus's flat. There's a lot of money in a tin box in the lower right drawer of his desk."

Dakin grinned. "Now, how would you know that?"

"A genie sure as hell didn't tell me. Unless I miss my guess, Nodo won't stray too far, if he can stray, without those pounds."

"And you?"

"I'll go over to Paul Hughes's office with him and get briefed. It would be a good idea to find out just what the hell brought Gerhard Rouse out of retirement."

"Good enough. And, Nick . . ."

"Yeah?"

"Sorry we didn't stay on Little's Garage . . . my fault."

"Not really."

Carter turned and walked toward Paul Hughes. In his mind he was cursing himself far more than Claude Dakin and Special Branch. It was he, and not them, who had spent the night between Lola's willing thighs.

"Lin, it's me."

"Luv, are ya comin' ta see me?"

"Yeah. I've had me a bit of a knock-up . . . not feelin' too well."

"At the club?"

"No . . . and not yer flat, either. Is yer mum still in Canada?"

"Yeh, me brother's talked her into stayin' another week."

"Listen, luv, here's what I want ya to do . . ." Nodo gasped as a gust of wind slapped ice pellets against his naked, charred side.

"Damon, are you all right?"

"To tell ya the truth, no. But I'll make it. I want you to get in yer car right now and drive up to London . . ."

"Damon, it's snowin' . . ."

"Dammit, I know it's snowin'. But I'm a hell of a lot closer to Surrey than I am to London, and I can't make it up there and back to Surrey as well, understand?"

"Yes, Damon."

"Good. Now, you've still got the key to my flat . . ."

"Aye, I do."

"In the bottom right-hand drawer of my desk . . ."

Paul Hughes drove up a winding, tree-lined drive to an enormous half-timbered Tudor-style mansion. It looked, bathed in snow, like a nineteenth-century postcard sent from the very rich to the equally rich.

"This is Brandeis?"

"Yes, it is, the corporate offices. The stables and guest cottages have also been converted into offices. You'll notice there is no sign. We just like to blend into the countryside."

They left the car to be parked by a uniformed guard, and climbed stone steps to a pair of massive oak doors that led into an enormous vestibule with polished parquet flooring. From there, Hughes led the way into a large room, furnished

Tudor style. There was a huge fireplace, a long, solid oak table, several chairs festooned with velvet-covered cushions, and a blood-red carpet under the whole.

"Your office?"

"Lord, no," Hughes replied with a chuckle. "Conference room. It's also used for board meetings."

A tray was set out with bottles and glasses. Hughes walked right to it, shedding his coat and Harris Tweed cap along the way.

"We have Scotch whisky, gin, and the makings of a martini, English or American."

"Scotch, neat."

Hughes poured gin for himself, and they moved to high-backed chairs in front of the fire.

"Well now, first of all, let me say I contacted our American offices straight away. They contacted the Pentagon and relayed back to me that I was to stay involved in this mess but turn the reins over to you. It seems you were sniffing up someone's behind who probably did this."

Carter nodded. "When I left London two hours ago, I wasn't sure."

"But you are now?"

"I am. His name is Gerhard Rouse. He has the reputation of pulling off the impossible, if the price is right."

Carter told him the whole story, from the initial spotting in Madrid through Europe to England. He also told Hughes about turning up Nodoramus after a lot of spade work, but he left out most of the time spent in Lola's flat above the club.

Carter liked the way the man listened to it all and digested it without breaking in with an opinion or question. When the Killmaster was finished, Hughes took both glasses back to the tray for refills.

"From the sound of it, this Rouse character is just a worker."

Carter nodded and accepted the fresh drink. "That's right. Whatever he took from your courier, he's going to pass on to someone else."

Hughes regained his seat. "The Reds."

Carter shrugged. "Could be. He's worked for them before."

"That could get very sticky. Pierce was bringing some top-secret papers and plans for some tests we're making next week."

Carter leaned forward. "Give me a rundown on that," he said. "Rouse doesn't work for peanuts, and, from the looks of it, neither does Nodoramus. This operation was well bank-rolled, so I'm assuming that the rewards are substantial."

"That's an understatement," Hughes replied. "As you probably know, the defense system of the future will be in space. To be more specific, in space stations. Until a few months ago, it was all theory and, pricewise, impractical. Recently that has changed. The reason it has changed is the perfections of a new method of gathering solar energy and converting it, not directly into a power source, but using it to create an antimagnetic field." He hesitated. "Am I losing you?"

Carter grinned. "Not if you keep it in layman's terms."

"I'll try. Remember, I'm only a glorified cop, like you."

"Go on," Carter said, thinking to himself, *If you only knew!*

"If these new methods work—and we firmly believe that they will—the cost of putting as many as twenty manned and armed stations in orbit would be a fraction of the current cost. As much as only ten percent. An additional plus is longevity and ease of maintenance."

"Such as?"

"Maintenance? Zero. I know it's hard to believe, but it's true."

"My God."

"Yes, it is a little mind-boggling. As to longevity, try about three hundred years."

"And that was what Pierce was carrying?"

Hughes nodded. "Plans for construction of the panels, the elements for the conversion, and the final staging plans for the stations' radar guidance system. It, too, is revolutionary, in that it can be programmed to detect a missile anywhere in the world in its very first stages of firing."

"So it could be destroyed right on the pad."

"Practically."

Carter lit a fresh cigarette and moved to the window. The snow had lightened up a little, but enough had already fallen to make the vast grounds of the estate pristine in a blanket of white. Just outside the window he saw a squirrel scamper down a tree, sniff the strange stuff at the bottom, and head back up.

"Smarter than we are," Carter murmured.

"What's that?"

"Nothing," Carter said, turning back to face the other man. "If these stations became a reality, how many years ahead of the Soviets would we be in that field?"

"Difficult to say. They've been working on a similar project for quite some time, but they're not faring too well."

"What's an educated guess?"

"Offhand, I'd say about fifteen years."

"In that time," Carter mused, "offensive weapons as we know them would be obsolete."

"That's about it."

Carter sighed. "I think I'd better get back to work. Can you lend me a car and driver to get back to London?"

"I can do better than that." Hughes picked up a phone and punched four numbers. "Brad, are you available? . . . Fine, I have a VIP who needs to get back to London rush-rush." He held his hand over the phone. "Company helicopter. Where would you like to go?"

"St. James's pad."

"Brad, St. James's pad . . . fine, we'll be over in a few minutes." He hung up and got to his feet. "The company wants me to stay on this, so I'd appreciate it if you would keep me informed."

"Will do," Carter replied, nodding. "In the meantime, I suggest you do a thorough check on everyone who knew Pierce's movements and what he would be carrying."

Hughes smiled enigmatically. "We've already started the process. Come along, I'll walk you out to the pad."

SEVEN

Lin followed Nodo's instructions to the letter. She drove her own car into London and parked in Knightsbridge. Then she walked down Brompton Road and found a cab.

"Where to, miss?"

"Hounslow, an' it's an extra fiver if ya makes it fast."

The driver blinked. Were his ears getting it all? A pretty Chinese girl, rigged out like a Chinese girl, and her accent was nearly as Cockney East End as his own.

The girl grinned. She could read his mind. They always looked at her like that.

"Me mother was Chinese, me father was a paddy from Yorkshire. Me last name's O'Keefe. Now can we get a move on?"

He had the taxi driver's knowledge of London. Up Brompton Road and on along Cromwell Road past Earl's Court, dodging other traffic, using his horn more than his brakes.

He got her to Hounslow in nineteen minutes. She paid, and walked quickly into Pekin Mews. When she reached the lower door of Nodo's flat, she already had her key out. The same for the upper door.

The screwdriver was right where Nodo said it would be. It took only seconds to pry the desk drawer open. She placed the tin box in a shopping bag and, on top of it, her photograph from the mantel and the Rolodex from beside the phone.

Leaving, she relocked both doors and took the rear alley behind the Mews. Normally, she would have walked out the front of the Mews directly onto Hounslow Road. Because she didn't, the two cars full of Special Branch men didn't see her.

Carter thanked the pilot for the ride, and made a beeline to a phone. Dakin was out and unavailable. Because of the short time span, the Killmaster guessed he was still at Nodo's flat.

In Lola's car heading toward Hounslow, he raged at himself for being constantly one step behind Rouse. Because of it, four men were dead, and somewhere there was another one probably dying.

There was a crowd of curiosity-seekers around the front of Nodoramus's flat. Carter flashed his credentials at the Special Branch man at the lower door and was waved on up to the flat.

Inside the apartment, there was a fingerprint team working and two other bored men cataloguing the flat's contents. Claude Dakin stood in the middle of the living room with a glum look on his face.

Before he spoke Carter knew that they were too late. "He beat us here."

"It's gone?"

Dakin nodded. "The woman downstairs heard him moving around up here not ten minutes before we arrived."

"Sir . . ."

Both men looked up. One of Dakin's men stood in the

bedroom doorway. He was holding a Ruger automatic rifle, a shotgun with eight inches sawed off the barrel, and a Baretta automatic.

"False ceiling in the closet."

"Anything else in there?" Carter asked.

"Nothing, sir."

"Catalogue them with everything else."

"Right."

Dakin turned to Carter with a half-smile. "I'm surprised you didn't find those when you found the tin box."

"So am I," Carter replied, and then sighed. "How are you doing with Harper Little?"

"I'm not. He's mum as a church mouse and he's screaming for a solicitor. Another eight hours and I'll have to let him call one."

"He could give us the license plates of the Rover and the Cortina. That would speed things up."

"It would, but our Mr. Little says he knows nothing. He's a hard one, been up a couple of times already. He knows we've got nothing on him and he's using it."

Carter mulled this over for a full minute. "Let him go."

"What?"

"Turn him loose, Claude."

"What have you got in mind?"

"You really don't want to know."

Dakin nodded. "I'll make a call."

Carter moved around the apartment and on into the bedroom. He took a hard look at the desk and the drawer that had been jimmied open.

One of Dakin's boys was dusting it for prints. "Bugger was in a hurry, wasn't he?"

Carter leaned over the man's shoulder so he could get a better look. The drawer had deep gouges in it where it had been pried open. "Yeah, he sure as hell was." He moved back into the living room. Dakin was just hanging up the phone.

"He'll be loose in about twenty minutes."

"I'll be in touch."

Carter drove back to the City at a leisurely pace. Near the Tower in the East End, he stopped in a pub and looked up the number of Little's Garage. Then he called Lola.

"Where's my car?"

"With me. I'm taking loving care of it."

"Where's my money?"

"You know something? You're a shrew."

"Business, luv, just business."

"I should charge you for sack time," Carter hissed.

"Ya can't. You're not that good," she cackled. "When am I gonna see you again?"

"Later. I've got a little errand to run."

She started to harangue him some more, but Carter hung up. He took a table by the window and ordered two beers from a weary-looking barmaid.

"What's the special?"

"Kidney pie."

"Bring it with the beers."

He ate slowly, and had coffee and brandy. When he finished, he moved to the bar and paid his tab with a twenty. When the girl gave him the change, he pushed it back across the bar.

"That's yours. Do me a favor?"

"Depends."

He took her pencil and pad. "Call this number and ask for Phil."

"And . . .?"

"That's it."

She shrugged and headed for the phone. Carter lit a cigarette and checked the weather. It had started snowing again, but lightly. The gray sky was bringing early darkness.

"Fella says there ain't no Phil there."

"Thanks." He turned from the bar.

"That's it?"

"That's it. Thanks." Leaving her staring quizzically at his back, he headed for the street.

He drove to Cable Street and parked a block from the garage. There was still a light on in the upstairs flat.

Two hours and half a pack of cigarettes later, the light went off.

Carter slouched in the seat and catnapped for another hour, then got out of the car.

The street was deserted as he crossed and darted into the doorway. It took a few minutes longer to pick the lock than it would usually take him because of the necessity for silence.

Inside, the only illumination came from a small night light in the office. He picked his way through the tools, benches, and vehicles to the sliding rear door. He opened it just enough to squeeze his body through, and hit the stairs to the second level.

Gingerly, he tried the knob and found the door locked. That wasn't surprising, considering Harp Little's last twenty-four hours.

The Killmaster took two steps back and made sure he nailed the door in one kick. The jamb ripped apart like tissue paper and the door burst inward, with Carter right behind it.

He leaped at the startled, groggy figure on the bed without a pause and came down, hard, on Little's gut with both feet. After the first crunch of contact, Carter tumbled off the bed and landed standing up.

Harp Little was gasping for air and coming after him. Carter was ready with both hands clenched together like a hammer. He swung with all the strength in his upper body, and knew the blow was solid by the sound of Little's nose cracking and the gush of blood down over his bare chest.

The Killmaster could have stopped there and started his questions, but he wanted the man in total fear and pain so there would be no waffling when it came to answers.

Carter's blow to the face had knocked Little clear over the bed. By the time the Killmaster followed, the other man was on his feet. He was flailing his arms, fighting for consciousness and trying to get some air past the blood that was gushing from his ruptured nose.

Carter grabbed him by the hair and yanked him forward to a bowing position. When the squirming body was just right, he stepped back and kicked him square in the center of his chest.

Little went limp and fell across the bed.

"Little! Harp Little!" Carter hissed, leaning forward until his face was just above the other man's.

"Uggg, who the hell . . ."

"Who I am doesn't matter, Little. I ask, you answer. Nodo had to run after the heist. Where would he run?"

Little gathered the strength to spit into Carter's face and swing an ineffectual right.

"Stupid bastard."

He crossed the room and tore the leg from a rickety chair. By the time he turned, Little was back on his feet, trying to get set for round two.

He never came close.

Carter danced just out of range, using the chair leg to systematically break the man's ribs.

Little finally crumpled to the floor and lay inert, a tub of lard mashed out of shape.

Carter took him by the hair and dragged him back up across the bed. He lay still, like a naked blob of blood and blubber.

The Killmaster turned on a lamp and ransacked the room until he found a pint of gin with about four fingers left in it. With the bottle in one hand, a cigarette in the other, and the chair leg propped beside him, he perched on the headboard and waited.

It took the better part of an hour before Little came around. He groaned a few times but moved only one eylid. The bloodshot orb stared up at Carter.

"I'll have you on charges," he croaked.

"Maybe, if you're alive. You see, Little, I don't give a shit if I kill you. You're no more than a piss-ant to me."

He picked up the chair leg for emphasis.

"All right, all right, you bloody bastard. Whaddaya wanna know?"

"The plate numbers on the Rover and the Cortina."

Little concentrated and then rattled them off. "The Rover belongs to a knob in Knightsbridge. Nodo nicked it just for the job. The Cortina was bought for the job all legal like, in a phony name. The both of them have nicked plates for the job."

"Where's Nodo?"

"I don't know, I swear. If the job went wrong, I wanted nothing to do with it. I got 'em the van and the Escort and the plates. Besides givin' 'em storage until it was go-time, I didn't have nothin' else to do with it."

"What about Rouse?"

"Who?"

"Gerhard Rouse."

"I don't know any Rouse. That was part of my deal. I see only Nodo. I don't know who else he got for the job."

Carter believed him. He hadn't gotten much beyond the

plate numbers and some statisfaction, but he was pretty sure he wasn't going to get anything else.

He tossed the chair leg into a corner and headed for the door. "I would suggest, Harp, that you get into another line of business. If you stay in your current one, you might come across me again."

He left the door open and went down the stairs. It took fifteen minutes of driving before he found a pay phone that worked. He gave Special Branch's twenty-four-hour number the plate numbers of the two cars, and hung up.

Back in Lola's car, he debated. It was nearly midnight. Should he return the car now and take a chance on hassling with her?

No.

He started the car and headed for the West End and the Charing Cross flat. He parked several blocks away out of security habit, and walked toward the flat.

The last block before the flat was parallel to Soho Square. He found himself running a gauntlet of streetwalkers.

"A tenner will get you a quick one, dearie!"

"What's a good-lookin' bloke like you doin' alone tonight?"

"Lookin' fer a date, luv?"

Most of them stayed in the shadows. A few would dart into the light just long enough to display the product.

Carter smiled and shook his head at them all. He was about to turn into the small street leading to the tall apartment house, when one of them got bolder. She slid her arm through his and walked with him.

"You like to catch young girl? . . . Not too much money?"

She was young and cute. Her makeup had been layered on with care to emphasize the exotic cast of her Asiatic features. The side slits in the skirt went clear up past her hips, exposing her legs. They were good legs for such a small girl, made longer by the spike heels of the smallest and most improbable pair of high heels Carter had ever seen.

Mistaking his slackening pace and concentrated stare as interest, she pulled the front panel of the dress aside with a smile.

She wore nothing beneath the dress.

"You like Vietnamese girl under Chinee dress?"

Carter pulled a wad of bills from his pocket, jammed a twenty-pound note into her hand, and sprinted for the building.

He cursed the elevator for being too slow and his trembling fingers getting the key into the lock. Inside, he dived for the phone.

"This is Washington, N3. I have to talk to Claude Dakin."

"Agent Dakin is not here, sir. It's nearly one in the morning."

"I know that. Give me his home number."

"I can't do that, sir."

"All right, dammit. It's pertaining to the case in Wales, the killing of the Brandeis courier and two other men."

"Yes, sir."

"I need access right now to the flat inventory of one Damon Nodoramus. It was taken this afternoon."

"I'm not allowed to give that out, sir."

"Shit . . ."

"Sir?"

"This is Priority One! You call Dakin at home and have him call N3 at this number. If he doesn't call in three minutes, I'll have your ass back pushing lager in a pub!"

He gave her the number and slammed the phone down. He built a scotch and paced until the phone rang.

"Claude?"

"Yes, it's Claude," came the sleepy reply. "Must you

terrorize poor little switchboard operators?"

"In this case, yes. Listen . . ."

"Do you realize it's one o'clock in the morning?"

"It's quarter past," Carter replied. "I just got a brainstorm. That desk drawer at Nodoramus's flat was pried open."

"Yes, it was. Probably with a screwdriver."

"And the guns in the back of the closet . . ."

"What about them?" Dakin asked.

"If Nodo himself had been there to get the tin box, he would have used his *key* on the drawer, not a damn screwdriver! I also think he would have taken at least one of the guns, probably the Beretta."

"Then someone made the pickup for him." The sleep was fading from Dakin's voice.

"Right. Remember I told you there was a Rolodex missing from the phone table?"

"I remember."

"Well, I just remembered something else missing. At least I didn't see it."

"Hold on, I've got a copy of the inventory in my briefcase." He was gone for less than a minute. "I'm back."

"There was a framed eight-by-ten photo on the mantel, in color. It was of a pretty Chinese girl in a satin cheongsam. It was inscribed with a message and the name Lin."

"It's not on the inventory."

"Claude, I just remembered that the girl was posing in front of a theatrical curtain, and there were footlights."

"A theater?"

"Or a club. Check the inventory for an ashtray on the phone table."

"It's here."

"Describe it."

"Silhouette of a naked woman. Written under that is *PENNY'S, QUEEN'S ROAD WEST, SURREY.*"

"Claude, I'll call you back from Surrey."

He quickly hung up and redialed.

"Lola's."

"Gimme Lola."

"She's busy."

"Tell her to get un-busy or she'll never get her thirteen hundred pounds."

With Lola, the mention of money was magic. She was on the line in seconds.

"If you stay in the U.K., National Telephone should be in the black by the end of next week."

"What do you know about a club in Surrey called Penny's?"

"I'm no bloody information service."

"You're back on the payroll."

"I've heard it's a little kinky. In the wee hours, they've been known to put on shows that would shock your granny out of her drawers."

"Put on your kinkiest outfit. We're going slumming."

EIGHT

Penny's was about as Carter had expected, large and dark. An outrageous membership fee got him by the harridan at the door. All the tables and booths were filled with people, but there were some empty stools along the bar. Carter topped one, ordered a whiskey neat, and watched the front door.

He and Lola had come up with a plan on the way down. It was simple and would probably work without a lot of fuss.

The heavyweight bouncer stood just inside the door. His suit hung loosely from his shoulders. He was all shoulders, narrow hips, no belly, and heavy thighs. His nose had been broken more than once. His blue eyes moved in slow sweeps around the club. Despite his face, his manner was mild and inconspicuous, but nothing was going to happen that he didn't see almost before it happened.

He walked in small circles near the door, and each time he passed the telephone booths he paused to feel inside the coin returns. It was the habit of a man who had once been a poor kid.

Then Lola entered. Carter chuckled to himself. She had done herself up in her kinkiest and tartiest. In a leather blouse cut to her navel and no bra, along with a leather miniskirt that covered nothing, she looked like a refugee from a bad porno movie.

She exchanged a few words with the heavyweight and he looked her over as if he could devour her in three bites. Satisfied, he pointed her to a bench and headed toward a door in the rear marked Office.

Carter exchanged a single glance with her, and spun on his stool to check out the rest of the room for his future act.

By the stage, where three pre-stripped strippers gyrated forlornly, three musicians—trumpet, drums, and piano— wailed.

Between Carter and the small stage there was an enormous Greek-looking man with a drooping mustache and soulful eyes that never left the dancers' bodies. Next to him was a little man with a big cloth cap and a cigarette stuck to his lower lip. Right by the stage sat a pair of young lovers. They, too, were concentrated on the dancers, and under the table they were playing with each other.

Carter spotted what he wanted just to the right of the lovers. There were two pretty brunettes with tight skirts, slender waists pinched tight by patent-leather belts, and satin blouses that strained tautly across jutting breasts.

They had both watched Carter from the moment he'd entered, and they watched even closer as he ordered a second drink and took out his well-filled wallet to pay for it.

Carter smiled. They smiled back and inclined their heads toward the empty chair at their table. Grabbing his drink, he staggered toward them. Halfway there, he was intercepted by a blond Amazon in an opaque plastic raincoat.

"You want to buy me a drink?" She unsnapped the raincoat and opened it. Underneath it she was as bare as the day she was born.

"I've got a date," Carter replied.

She refastened the raincoat and drifted toward the Greek. Carter covered the rest of the distance to the brunettes and took the empty chair.

"Buy you ladies a drink?"

"Champagne," they said as one, and it appeared as if by magic.

Out of the corner of his eye he saw the bouncer escorting Lola toward the office. He glanced at his watch and decided ten minutes would be about right.

"What do you fine-looking ladies do?"

Together they said, "We're shopgirls, but we work on the side."

Carter grinned. "Don't you mean on your backs?"

They even giggled together.

Carter sipped his drink and made a lewd small talk. As the minutes passed, he began to notice something strange. It was as if everyone were waiting for something big to happen. It was like a countdown.

Suddenly the whole place grew quiet. The lights dimmed. A spot came up on stage, and from between the curtains a bed rolled out. On it was a beautiful naked girl. In time to the pulsating beat of the music, she was doing a solo of working herself into a state of simulated passion.

"It's showtime!" the brunettes said.

Carter was about to reply, when a curly-haired giant came from behind the curtains. He wore only a jockstrap as he pranced and posed around the stage.

After a few minutes of this, he dropped the jockstrap and climbed onto the bed.

"Some show," Carter murmured.

"You better believe it," the brunettes replied, their four eyes glued to the stage.

Carter checked his watch. It was time for his own show. He stood and walked to the stage.

"Sin!" he shouted. "This place is full of sin and you are all sinners . . ."

Penny was about two hundred and twenty pounds in a satin tent. A foot-high, foot-wide blond wig covered her head and part of a hard face layered with a pound and a half of makeup.

Lola chewed her gum and took a seat.

"What's yer name, dearie?"

"Lily."

"Anybody to recommend ya?"

Lola nodded. "Lin."

"Lin who?"

Lola shrugged. "Who has last names?"

"The girls that work fer me do, luvvy. I don't hire nobody that's been in the nick . . ."

Lola concentrated on manufacturing an answer, but found it wasn't necessary when all hell broke loose in the main room.

"Oh, Christ," Penny wailed, heaving her bulk from the chair, "some horny bastard probably tryin' to get into the act again. S'cuse me."

She sailed like an ocean liner through the door, and Lola attacked the desk.

She found the payroll ledger under some other papers in the middle drawer.

"Repent!" Carter shouted as he backpedaled and darted among the tables, always just ahead of the bouncer. "Repent, or mark me, you will burn in hell!"

The couple on the stage were both standing by the bed staring in stark, naked amazement. The patrons were split. Half of them were laughing like hell, and the other half were cursing him for busting up the spectacle.

It was on his third go-round of the room when Carter saw the lady tank emerge from the office. He maneuvered so she could head him off. And she did, one hand around the back of his neck and the other at his belt.

"Just what the hell do ya think you're doin', mate?" she thundered.

"Saving souls, madam, saving souls," he replied solemnly.

"Yer arse!"

She yanked up on his belt, bringing his pants tight into his crotch. He yelped and went limp. By this time the bouncer had arrived and got him in a neck lock.

"Boot him!" the tank rasped.

Carter let himself be piloted through the room, but he kept up his exhortations to one and all.

"The fruits of sin are hell! Let its fires consume this place of flesh and evil! Follow me, my flock! Sir Nick of Canterbury will . . ."

By this time he was sailing through the door and sliding across the sidewalk. He waited until the door slammed behind him, and then stood and brushed the snow from his knees and elbows.

Whistling, he walked to the car, climbed in, and lit a cigarette.

About ten minutes later, Lola joined him. "I'm in the wrong racket," she cried. "She says I could make fifteen hundred quid a week!"

"You're making that in two days and it's nice clean work," Carter grinned. "Give."

"The only Lin in the address book was Lin O'Keefe. That doesn't sound very Chinese."

"It's all we've got. Where?"

"Sixteen Cadbury Road, flat Four."

Carter checked a Surrey map and dropped the car into gear.

Cadbury Road was in a run-down, workingman's section of identical brick flats. There wasn't a light on in the neighborhood.

"Honk twice if there's any movement around. Three if something starts into the building."

Lola nodded and slouched down in the seat so she could see the building's entrance but no one could see her. Carter slipped the Luger into his belt and trotted across the street.

Apartment Four was the top right. He rapped gently on the door. When there was no answer, he rapped again, and when the other side was still quiet, he went to work with a credit card on the lock.

Damon Nodoramus obviously didn't share much of his wealth with his girl friend. The place was a dump.

The single room was dark save for a little street light making its way through a pair of shoddy, pull-down shades. There was an unmade bed, a round table and a single straight-backed chair, and a television set on top of a packing crate covered with an old silk shawl. Along one wall there was a sink that also served as a washbasin, a two-burner gas cooker, and some open wooden shelves that held a few dishes and cutlery.

Carter flicked a switch that lit a hanging bulb of low wattage, shrouded in something that looked like a very soiled beaded handbag.

There were no cooking smells, and despite bottles of cheap perfume everywhere, Carter could detect no scent in the air. If the woman used a tenth of what was displayed, her scent would have remained in the air for at least six or seven hours.

Shoved under the bed was a telephone answering machine. Carter tugged it out, rewound the announcement tape, and hit "Play."

"Hi, this is Lin. I'll be outta the flat fer a few days and at me mum's. If ya want to leave a message, wait 'til the beep sounds off an' I'll call ya back in a few days."

He searched for ten minutes but could find no address book in the flat. He turned to the local directory. There were nine O'Keefes.

The first five had never heard of Lin and cursed him for calling at such an hour. The sixth was the number from which he was calling.

The seventh was answered by a young, frightened woman.

"Lin?"

"Yeah, who's this?"

"My name is Carter, Lin. I'm an American."

"Whaddaya want? I—"

"Don't hang up, Lin. I know Nodo is there with you. Can he talk?"

"You're daft! I don't know—"

"Lin, calm down. I know he's in a bad way. I'm not a copper. I want to talk to him."

Carter could hear a mumbled discussion through the girl's hand over the mouthpiece, and then a gruff but weak voice.

"Yeah, whaddaya want?"

"Nodo?"

"It's you who wants to talk, talk."

"Okay. I know about you, about Rouse, and about the heist."

"Go on."

"I also know about the tin box Lin fetched from your flat, and what was in it. But I don't care about that, or you. I want what the courier was carrying. I want Rouse."

There was a full minute of silence before the other man

spoke again. "How do I know I can trust you?"

"You don't. I can bust in there and blow you and the girl to hell, or I can walk in there and talk. What's it to be?"

Another long silence. "All right. Come ahead."

The little cottage was bleak in the early-morning grayness. The woman who answered the bell was small, dark-haired, and pretty. She was also very frightened.

"You're Carter?"

He nodded. "This is Lola."

"Come in." They stepped inside. "He's in there, an' ya better not try nothin'. He's got a gun, he has."

"How bad is he?" Carter asked.

She swallowed hard and averted her eyes. "He's bad, and he won't go to a hospital."

With his eyes, Carter told Lola to watch her, and he walked into the bedroom.

Nodo was propped up in the bed on pillows, a sheet pulled to his waist. A .32 was in his lap, held in two shaky hands.

His head, half of his face and body, and one arm were swathed in blood-darkened bandages. The room smelled of burned and decaying flesh.

"Sit there, where I can see ya."

Carter sat. Nodo's one eye was bloodshot and wild. Even from a distance of six feet Carter could tell that the man was on his last legs.

"You're dying, Nodo. Even if you got to a hospital you wouldn't make it."

"Don't you think I bloody well know that!"

"I want to make a deal," Carter said calmly.

"Shit, what kind of a deal can ya make with a dead man?"

"None. But I can make one with a live woman. Do you care about Lin at all?"

His eye wavered and then came back to fix on Carter. "Never did before. Maybe I do, now."

"I can fix it so she keeps your money."

Nodo laughed and then squirmed in agony. "Ain't that a fat one . . ."

"Yeah, it is. I can also get you a little revenge. Rouse killed your mate, didn't he?"

"Yeah, the bloody bastard shot Vrain like a dog!"

"I want Rouse, Nodo."

He thought about this for quite a while, and while he thought the revolver dropped. Carter reached over and lifted it, by the barrel, from his lap.

"I never did trust him, ya know."

"Rouse?"

"Yeah. He's a shifty devil."

"Where can I find him?"

"When we finished the job, he was gonna drive the Rover straight to Gatwick and fly out fer France."

"You're sure it was France?"

Nodo nodded his head slightly. "But I don't think he was goin', leastwise not right away."

"How do you know that?"

"Like I say, I didn't trust him all the way. Fer the three days he was here, he told me he was stayin' in London. But he wasn't. Me and Vrain followed him so if he tried to cross us, we'd know where we could find him."

"Where was he staying?"

"You call 'em mobile homes or trailers in America. Over here we call 'em caravans. He's got one rented in Thorton Cove, just west of Brighton. They's six of 'em spread out in a grove of trees. His is number Three. It's the only one that's all silver-colored. Me guess is, he'll hang out there fer a while before he tries to get out of the country."

"Anything else?"

"Yeah. He called about four times a day checkin' in with the bloke that hired him. Sometimes he'd do it from me flat. I never got the whole number, but the area call numbers was seven-seven-one. That's in France someplace."

Carter stood. "Can you move?"

"A little."

"Then have the girl get you out of here so the police don't connect you with her."

Nodo smiled. "You're a cold bastard, ain't ya."

"That I am," Carter said, and walked from the room. "He wants to see you."

The girl darted into the bedroom and Carter grabbed Lola's hand. "C'mon."

"What now?"

"First a phone call, then Brighton."

It was false dawn, not much lighter than it had been an hour before, but light enough to see. One by one, Dakin's men had quietly awakened the occupants of the nearby caravans and gotten them out of the way.

Now there were eight of them, all heavily armed, ranged through the trees in a wide circle around number Three. A Mini was parked at the door of the trailer, and there were no lights. Carter and Dakin were crouched in a hedgerow about twenty yards away.

"We're set," Dakin whispered.

Carter nodded and raised the bull horn to his lips.

"Rouse! Gerhard Rouse! This is Nick Carter, American Intelligence. You are surrounded by British Special Branch. You have two minutes to come out with your hands on your head or we will take the caravan!"

The bull horn boomed through the still morning air, carrying all the way to the ocean. On a ridge running along the ocean, an old, gray-haired woman straddled a bicycle and listened to the shouted command, and nodded.

The wind whipped at her coat, revealing strikingly long, attractive legs as she lifted a camera equipped with a high-powered zoom lens to her eye.

As Carter's voice boomed a second time on the bull horn, the camera began to click. When the woman was sure she had several good close-ups of the American's face, she let the camera fall to her chest. Then she turned the bike on the trail and began riding away. Two miles away, in Brighton Harbor, there would be a motor launch that would take her along the coast to Folkestone. There she would catch the ferry to Calais, where she would stay the night.

It was good, Solange thought, that she had pumped Rouse first and found out that an American agent had been trailing him across Europe.

It was luck that she had spotted the cars full of men coming out of Brighton, and guessed their destination. Charmont would want to keep tabs on this Nick Carter, she was sure.

"It's been half hour," Carter growled. "I'm going in."

He duck walked across the open ground to the safety of the Mini. When there was no sign of life and he had drawn no fire, he rolled to the steps leading up to the door. Carefully, he slid up the side of the trailer and went to work.

By the time it clicked open, Dakin was at his side, his service revolver in his hand. Carter threw the door open and they both rolled in, Dakin covering the small living room, Carter's Luger on the narrow hallway leading to the other end.

Carter, staying low, moved toward the bedroom past a table, two padded benches, and the usual built-in stove and sink.

"Claude . . ."

"Yes?"

"Back here."

Gerhard Rouse lay sprawled across the bed. He was naked and his throat was cut almost from ear to ear. His head was tilted back, and all the muscles, tendons, and veins were visible, white now in the quiet of death. Dark red coagulated blood covered the upper part of his body and spread across the sheet, as though someone had poured a bucket of rust-colored paint over him.

"That him?"

Carter nodded. "Gerhard Rouse. Whoever got him was good. He was a careful man."

Dakin moved forward and probed the man's neck and armpits with his fingers. "Probably a little more than an hour."

Carter nodded. "Bring your team in, although I doubt if they'll find anything."

Dakin went to the door and issued orders while Carter moved around the tiny bedroom. There were paperback books and magazines scattered on the floor by the bed, and two good-sized ashtrays were full of cigarette butts.

Obviously, Rouse had spent a considerable bit of time in the caravan.

He stooped and checked under the bed. Nothing but dust. As he came back up, he paused, then leaned toward the space beside Rouse's body. He sniffed several times before he could be sure of what his nostrils told him.

Jasmine . . . body powder or perfume, or both.

He moved into the bathroom. The floor of the tiny shower was wet. Two towels with faint smudges of diluted blood were thrown carelessly on the floor.

Dakin came by.

"Claude, it was a woman."

"What?"

Carter explained, and added, "She got him into the sack, into the position, and then it was bye-bye Gerhard Rouse."

"Jesus."

"Yeah. I'd bet my pension on it," Carter growled. "It would fit, the only way Rouse would be vulnerable."

The two Special Branch teams went to work. Carter and Dakin continued to search. They found the courier's bag stuffed behind the couch in the living room.

The middle part, the briefcase section, was empty.

NINE

In the third-floor conference room of the Soviet embassy in Paris, Arkady Tarkovsky flipped through the envelopes in the pouch that had arrived that night from Moscow. There were fourteen envelopes. He selected three marked Top Secret.

From the lining of his jacket he took a microscopically thin pair of tweezers. He picked up the first envelope and carefully inserted the tweezers under one corner of the flap without creating so much as a roll in the paper. This done, he deftly rotated them around and around.

When the fine tongs were extracted from the envelope, a single sheet of onion skin was wrapped tightly around them. When the onion skin was unwrapped and spread on the desk, Tarkovsky removed his right shoe.

He twisted the heel to the side and peeled back the heel pad on the inside of the shoe. He was now looking through the lens of a Japanese-made Isoba subminiature camera. He trained the shoe over the page and snapped the shutter twice. The internal gears of the camera were powered by a microchip battery, and they were made of fishing line so the camera made no sound.

Just as carefully as he had extracted the sheet, he returned it to the envelope. He then performed the same task with the other two envelopes marked Top Secret, and returned them to the bag. When his tools were again secreted, he picked up the bag and mounted the stairs to the fourth-floor file room.

"The evening dispatches, comrade," Tarkovsky said, handing over the bag.

"Thank you, Arkady. You're off?"

Tarkovsky smiled. "The bit of fluff I mentioned in Montmartre? I think tonight is the night."

The file clerk laughed. "I think I hate all of you who don't have to live in the compound."

When the door closed behind Arkady Tarkovsky, the clerk picked up a phone and dialed three numbers. It was answered at once.

"He was sixteen minutes from the car to here."

"Then it's a drop."

"That's the way he's been working it," the clerk said. "He's coming down now."

"*Da*." The line went dead.

The clerk emptied the pouch. The eleven routine envelopes he filed in the boxes of the embassy officers to which they had been assigned. The three marked Top Secret he carelessly dropped into a shredder.

Then he ran a razor-thin, equally sharp knife along the lower stitching of the bag. From this narrow compartment he withdrew five envelopes marked Top Secret—*Rezident*.

These he filed in their proper lock box, and then strolled away to have himself a cup of tea.

The traffic across the width of Paris was heavy. The driver of the fifth cab Arkady Tarkovsky had taken since leaving the embassy cursed steadily, taking a craftsman's care never to repeat an obscenity, as he wound through the cars.

"The *périphérique* would have been easier, monsieur."

"I realize that. I prefer the back streets."

Ten minutes later, the ride ended and the driver thanked his passenger for an ample tip.

"Monsieur, you know this is the Algerian section, very dangerous."

The Russian shrugged and stepped from the cab. He waited until it had pulled away, and then he seemingly began to wander aimlessly through the tiny back streets and alleys.

"Monsieur, you want young girl, virgin . . . ?"

"You want good hashish . . . Morocco? Make your woman do crazy things for you!"

A young girl with pin-dot pupils in her eyes offered him oral sex under a fire escape. A half block farther on, he got the same offer from a young boy in the same condition.

Tarkovsky ignored them and walked on, keeping a wary eye over his shoulder. He crossed Vincennes where it cut through Rue Napoleon. Some tough-looking Algerian youths gave him a hard-eyed appraisal as he turned into Allée Parque, but they fell back when he stared them down.

Number 17 Allée Parque was the last building on the dead end. It was an eighteenth-century graystone, tall, narrow, and imposing. The flat he wanted was on the second floor.

He took a last look up and down the street, and rang the bell. A buzzer sounded at once and he stepped into the dark hallway.

The door of 2B was open a crack. When Tarkovsky reached it, the door opened wide. He darted inside and it was immediately closed behind him.

"You were careful?"

"Always," Tarkovsky replied.

The room's occupant had a gap between his two upper front teeth that made his speech whistle. He wore dirty blue jeans, a gray sweatshirt, and worn loafers with no socks. He was about forty, with a narrow, hollow-cheeked face, sparse blond hair, and haunted eyes behind thick glasses that gave him the appearance of a seedy intellectual.

His name was Marcel du Court, and he had been a top CIA operative in France for nine years.

The Frenchman received the Russian curtly, with a nod instead of a handshake. He turned to light a small lamp while Tarkovsky removed his shoe. Carefully, he released two catches and the heel came off in his hand. Seconds later, he had removed the camera unit.

"Your hands are shaking, Arkady."

"It has been a difficult week, so many dispatches," the Russian replied.

Marcel du Court noted the deepening lines of worry around the Russian's eyes, and the beads of sweat that had popped out on his forehead and upper lip. Tarkovsky couldn't be more than thirty-five, and he looked hard-muscled and very fit, possibly too much so, like an over-trained athlete.

But the pressure of his dual life for the last year was beginning to register. He exuded the aura of a watch that has been wound too tight. If someone—or something—opened the back and the tight mainspring snapped out, the inner works would be strewn all over hell.

In his years with the Company, du Court had handled many, many agents. He had seen a few of them crack under the strain.

Arkady Tarkovsky was beginning to show those same signs.

The Russian handed over the camera with the exposed

film in its entirety. Du Court handed him a new unit, which he inserted back in the heel.

Du Court lit a heavy Turkish cigarette and, almost at once, Tarkovsky began coughing. "Christ, how can you smoke that filth?" he cried.

The Frenchman inhaled and blew the smoke directly at the other man. "If I were a Russian and started a sentance with the word 'Christ,' I don't think I would comment about another's filthy habit. Indulge me my Turkish tobacco and I'll let you backslide with Jesus."

"You know," Tarkovsky sighed, "I really don't like you very much."

"Neither of us is in a popularity contest, Arkady. You are well paid for what you bring us."

"I earn it."

Du Court shrugged. "Perhaps. In these days, greed is a universal ideal. I make no judgments. I, like you, am merely a courier." He bounced the tiny camera in his hand. "How many dispatches?"

"Three."

"Anything you can add to them?"

"One is a notation that the spring maneuvers in East Germany and Poland will be moved up one week this year."

The Frenchman nodded. "We probably have that from ten or twelve sources. Go on!"

"A request to look further into the blackmailing of Marshal LeFrond's wife's drinking problem. There may be some chance of blackmail there."

"Probably not," du Court snorted. "The old whore's liver will most likely blow up before a scheme can be implemented. And the third?"

"Permission for Boris Arksanov to go ahead on an intelligence purchase. His wife Bella is to make the exchange on the fourteenth of this month."

"Any comments?"

Tarkovsky thought for a moment. "Only that it is odd that she would make the exchange, instead of Arksanov."

"Why?"

"Because the amount is large, ten million Swiss francs, in gold."

Du Court's eyes opened wide with new interest. "Any details on the place of exchange, or the buyer?"

"None."

"Very well, Arkady. I'll wait for your next signal."

It was a dismissal, and Tarkovsky welcomed it. He scurried down the stairs and walked several blocks before hailing a cab.

"Rue Salene, number Twelve, in Montmartre."

In his agitated state, Tarkovsky didn't see the Paris *Poste* van fall in behind the taxi and follow it for nearly a mile. When the van fell away, a motorcyclist with QUIK, QUIK DELIVERY on his helmet took its place.

The motorcyclist didn't veer away until Tarkovsky's destination—his mistress's flat on Rue Salene—was confirmed.

Boris Arksanov sat in his sumptuous office and stared absently through the tall windows at the lights of Paris. In his hand was a tall glass of vodka. Unlike many of his comrades, Arksanov sipped his vodka instead of throwing it back like a barbarian.

Boris Arksanov did everything in moderation.

"Come in," he growled in response to a rap on the door.

"We have the report on Tarkovsky. He made the drop as usual, and taxied on to Montmartre."

"And the Frenchman?"

"He left Allée Parque about a half hour later. There was no need to follow him. We had a man waiting in surveillance across from the bakery. The CIA agent went directly there."

"Good, good."

Boris Arksanov's eyes narrowed. He sat back in the swivel chair and put the tips of his long fingers together.

"And what do we have from London?"

"The man Rouse was murdered in Brighton."

"Then the documents are on the way to Monsieur Charmont. What of the American agent, Carter?"

"Still in London."

Arksanov stood. He was a tall, gaunt man, and he had a permanent stoop as though the ceiling of the room were three inches too low for his height.

"Will there be anything else, comrade?"

"No, not for now. Keep the airports covered for this Carter. We'll let the Americans make the next move."

TEN

When the call finally came, Carter was ready to climb the walls of the Charing Cross flat. It had been seven days since the heist and the discovery of Rouse's body.

The instructions from Hawk in Washington had been to sit tight until something developed. Sitting tight was hard to do. Claude Dakin had the ball in England now, and there was little new on that end. Lola was bored with no action and no profit, so she had crawled back into her hole.

Carter drank and ate, saw some shows, and was generally bored.

The call came around noon of the seventh day.

"Fly open into Geneva, then get lost on the way to Lausanne. Got it?"

"Got it," Carter replied.

"Check into the Pension St. Pierre in Lausanne. The meet is being set up now. You'll be contacted at the pension. Use your Charles Coldeck passport."

Carter phoned for a reservation on the one-thirty flight, and packed light—one of the things he did often, in case everything had to be left. Just before leaving the flat, he called Lola.

"I'm leaving."

"Bully."

"It was fun."

A pause. "Yeah, it was. Gimme a call when you can afford me again."

"God, you're a bitch."

"I know, but do give me a call."

"I will."

He cabbed to Gatwick and just made the flight. Two scotches later, Lac Léman came up under the port wing and the plane set down at Cointrin Airport in Geneva.

Carter claimed his bag and went through customs in a breeze. He taxied to the Hotel des Tourelles, checked in, and was taken up to his room. The bellboy checked everything and then stood in front of Carter waiting for his reward.

He was tall, blond, and looked like a skier. He also had a look in his blue eyes that Carter spotted as sharp.

"I've got a problem."

"Anything to help, monsieur."

Carter took out two crisp American hundred-dollar bills and smoothed them on the coffee table. "I've got an itch and a nosy wife."

The kid smiled and Carter knew he had a winner.

"Oui, monsieur."

"This evening, I want you to order me a fine dinner, deliver it yourself, and eat it yourself. Understand?"

"I understand."

"Tomorrow morning, I want breakfast the same, and if I'm not back for lunch, it's the same deal." He pushed the two bills across the table and they disappeared. "Is there a quiet, inconspicuous way out of the hotel?"

The young man nodded. "Behind the rear stairs, a white door. It goes through the laundry room." He checked his watch. "It will be empty in about an hour."

"Good. Add a bottle of Chivas to that, and some ice. And bring it up immediately."

Carter flipped him another twenty and the young man slipped from the room. Carter took off his jacket and shirt and shaved while he was waiting. The whiskey arrived just as he came out of the bathroom. He made a stiff one, returned to the bathroom and a long, hot shower.

Another drink took him through unpacking and dressing. By that time he figured the laundry room would be empty.

It was. He scooted through the laundry room and up the alley to the Boulevard James-Fazy. On the corner, he grabbed a cab.

"Hotel Tor."

The driver stopped at the front entrance. Carter paid him, entered the hotel, and walked to the bar. He ordered a drink and dropped a ten-franc note on the bar. One sip and he headed for the men's room and a telephone.

One quick call and he had the departure time for the next train to Lausanne.

He exited by the side door to Rue Levrier and grabbed a cab to the Petit Palais. There, he checked out Renoir and Picasso for a half hour, and caught a bus to Gare Cornavin.

"One way to Bern, please."

"*Oui, monsieur.*"

Carter hung back in the crowd, smoking until one minute before the train pulled out. Then he walked through the barrier and waited until the guard had closed all the doors and the train began to move before he jumped aboard.

He was the last one on the train, and that was the way he wanted it.

The bed was feather soft in the Pension St. Pierre, and Carter took advantage of it. When the light tap came on his door, it was dark outside the windows.

"Yes?"

"Concierge, *monsieur*."

Carter opened the door and the man handed him a plain white envelope. "This just came, *monsieur*."

"*Merci*."

The envelope contained a key and a typewritten note: *Blue Cortina, Lic. A76-39, in the cathedral lot. Midnight, Château Les Barecottes, 3 kilometers N. Le Brassus. There are signs.*

Carter knew roughly where the village of Le Brassus was, but he checked a map to be sure. When he was positive of the route and the streets out of Lausanne, he left the pension.

It was a five-minute walk up the canal to the cathedral. The parking lot was on the water side, and the Cortina was one of three cars there.

Five minutes later he cleared the city and took a small two-lane asphalt west to Lac de Joux, where he would turn south to Le Brassus.

The moon was full with a slightly green tinge. It was a crisp, cloudless night that allowed the lunar glow to bathe the magnificence of the landscape. Away from the lights of the city, it was like driving in muted sunshine behind dark glasses.

In this area, the ski-and-crutch brigade retired early, so there was little traffic on the road. He made Lac de Joux without having to slow down once. Cutting south, he skirted the lake and passed through a tiny village, its occupants long since in bed. In seconds, he was back in the open country dotted with small farms and vineyards. The Cortina sighed along quiet, narrow lanes and roared through tunnels cut out of solid granite.

When he saw a sign, LE BRASSUS—5 KMS, he slowed. Two kilometers farther on, he saw a peeling white arrow with block letters, LES BARECOTTES.

A hundred yards up a narrow lane, he turned between two cement stiles with stone lions on top, and climbed to the château.

It was an impressive four-story chalet-type building set on a high knoll. It gleamed in the night sky high above a small parking area.

Carter slid the Cortina to a stop and killed the engine. He was just stepping from the car when a tall figure in a heavy coat and fur hat appeared like a panther out of the shadows.

"Hello, Nick."

Carter recognized the voice. It belonged to Neil Griffin, one of David Hawk's constant shadows. He knew that Gig Clark, the second shadow, would be close by.

"Neil. Must be quite a wing-ding if the old man himself flew over."

Griffin chuckled. "Must be. Lots of very important heads up there."

"I can hardly wait," Carter growled, and climbed the winding stone steps toward a pair of massive wooden doors.

He felt alone in a deserted place. Only a few dim lights muted by drawn curtains shone through the windows.

He was about to knock, when one of the doors opened and David Hawk's bulk filled the opening. His suit looked well traveled, which was unusual, but the cloud of gray cigar smoke suspended around his white-haired head was a reassuring constant.

"Nick."

"Sir."

"This way."

David Hawk had a habit of saying what was necessary and little else. The fact that he had answered the door himself told Carter that the château was a one-night stand, and it had probably been arranged in a hurry. No time to check out a staff.

Carter followed him into a high-ceilinged, wood-paneled room that could best be described as barren rustic. There were several high-backed leather-covered chairs around the wall, and a sideboard with a tray of cups and saucers and a coffeemaker. The only other furniture was a long table and a few chairs, all but two full.

Carter recognized Paul Hughes, the Brandeis security chief, John Starkey, AXE's liaison with the president, and Burt Esterman, the liaison man between AXE and the CIA.

The fourth man, slumped at the head of the table, Carter didn't know.

David Hawk wasted no time. "I think you know everyone, Nick, except Arthur Brandeis. Mr. Brandeis, our top agent, Nick Carter."

The head of Brandeis Limited was about fifty, a tired fifty. Like Hawk's, his four-hundred-dollar pinstripe looked rumpled from traveling. He had a wide pale forehead, dark wavy hair cunningly styled to hide a balding head, a sharp nose, pink at its tip, a red, small mouth that somehow looked mean but which may have been only firm, a bony chin that managed to appear ambitious, and dark, flickering eyes that looked as though they seldom gave anything away.

They probably didn't, Carter mused dryly. That's how millionaires became multimillionaires.

Carter shook hands, and when Hawk took the head of the table opposite Brandeis, he took the only empty chair, at the chief of AXE's right.

"Coffee, Nick?"

"No, thanks."

"I thought not. Scotch later. All right, let's get down to it. Starkey is here because the President has been informed and wants an hourly briefing. Burt is here because the CIA is already partway in on what's gone before. Mr. Hughes and Mr. Brandeis are here because they need to know how we're going to pull their asses out of the fire."

Another attribute of Hawk was bluntness. Carter lit a cigarette to hide a smile.

"Burt, brief Nick."

"Yes, sir." Esterman ruffled some papers and slid one to Carter. "This is a copy of a page lifted from the diplomatic bag at the Soviet embassy six days ago. Comments by the Company's mole made to his control are typed at the bottom. They turn out to be important."

"How good is the mole?" Carter asked.

"Not gold, but good. He's been there a little more than a year, and so far everything he's passed has been good."

Carter scanned the sheet and looked up. "Ten million Swiss? They are buying something big."

"You bet your ass they are," Hawk growled. "A fifteen-year skip in research."

Carter looked at Arthur Brandeis, and the man winced.

Esterman continued. "The Company has some other lines into the embassy, as well as a few feeders out of Moscow that helped on this. For a day or two they came up with nothing. Then they did some digging on the wife."

"Bella Arksanova?"

"Right. Boris is the Paris *rezident*. He's a full colonel, and he's good. His wife also ranks right up there. She's a major in the KGB, and often backs up her husband. The Company has a good profile on her. She's outgoing, gregarious, and she has high-level friends in every country where she and her husband have operated. She also has quite a record for philanthropy and worldwide charity, particularly in Third World countries. You might call her a hard-core social butterfly if you didn't know the whole story."

Here, Esterman paused to sip his coffee. After he had dug through a few more papers, he spoke again.

"Through idle gossip, the press, and some inside information, we managed to obtain Bella Arksanova's schedule for the next two months. On the weekend of the thirteenth and the fourteenth, she's attending a masquerade ball for charity."

"Where?" Carter asked.

"At the Château Charmont, near Arles on the Rhône River. We think that's where the exchange is going to be made."

"And she's picking up the papers hijacked from the Brandeis courier?" Carter asked.

Hawk growled, "There's not a damn thing out there right now that's worth a fraction of that kind of asking price except those documents. And there's another reason we think this is the big one. John?"

John Starkey leaned across the table. "Nick, it isn't common knowledge outside the State Department, but the owner of Château Charmont, René Charmont, has been a bone of contention between us and the French government for some time. We have proof that it was Charmont who played go-between for French arms manufacturers to Iran, Iraq, and a half-dozen other countries when they were under worldwide embargo. He's also been known to broker huge shipments of arms himself, as well as hijacking them."

"Busy man," Carter quipped.

"That's just the tip of the iceberg," Esterman continued. "In the last few years, we think he's also behind a lot of intelligence pilfering. And his major buyer is Moscow."

Carter gritted his teeth. "And the French do nothing?"

"They have a problem. Besides Charmont knowing where a lot of bodies are buried, he's the darling of café society and the ultrarich. He has status, not only in France, but all over Europe and even in the U.S. His many charity events have pumped millions into Third World economies.''

Carter mashed out his cigarette and stood. ''I think I'll have that coffee after all.''

It was Hawk's turn as Carter moved to the sideboard. ''An open assault on Charmont is out of the question, Nick. If we want to get Charmont out of the way for good, and recover the information these two gentlemen pissed away with lousy security, we'll have to do it by the back door.''

''Okay, I'll bite. What the hell's the back door? But first, where's the brandy?''

''Shelf underneath,'' Hawk chuckled. ''You lasted quite a while. The back door is an engineered robbery.''

Carter made the coffee half and half, and returned to his chair. ''I get me a few helpers and play Bonnie and Clyde?''

''Exactly,'' Hawk said, nodding. ''We want no international incidents, so there must be no connection. You'll be completely on your own. Not even your front money will come from us. Mr. Brandeis will supply that out of one of his foreign accounts.''

Hawk paused and tossed a German passport across the table. Carter opened it and read statistics that pretty well matched his own, right down to the age. His photo had already been laminated inside, and the name was Rolf Grottman.

''It's real,'' Hawk said. ''Grottman was a thief, and a damn good one. He pulled the London airport heist a few years ago, as well as the big tunneling job into Crédit National in Nice, and a three-million-dollar payroll robbery in San Francisco.''

''You said 'was'?''

''He died in Coravelle Prison in Spain four days ago. He was buried under the name of Martinez, and Grottman was granted a full pardon for all past sins. He's free as a bird.

If you'll notice, there's an entry stamp into Switzerland two days ago. The minute you leave your hotel in Geneva, you can be Rolf Grottman.''

Carter smiled. ''You work fast.''

Hawk shrugged. ''Desperate situations, desperate measures. You'll need five, maybe six men. It's up to you how you want to handle it. How you get them, and where you get them, is also up to you. Just make sure that none of them ever knows your real identity or your connections. Remember, Nick, it must look like a robbery, just a bunch of thieves on a big heist.''

Carter mused for a moment. ''Sir, I'd like to depart on one person. I'll need somebody to watch my back. Also, that someone should fit with the rest. It's a woman.''

''Can she be trusted?''

''Once, she couldn't,'' Carter replied. ''She can now.''

''You're sure?''

''I'm sure. She knows I'll kill her if there's any doubt.''

''I'll take your word for it,'' Hawk said. ''Brandeis?''

Arthur Brandeis came out of his stupor and cleared his throat. ''I have alloted one hundred thousand dollars in various currencies.''

Paul Hughes jumped in. ''Mr. Brandeis has made a mistake, Nick. That's one hundred and fifty thousand. I'll have it delivered anyplace you say.''

''Cheap enough to save your ass,'' Hawk said.

Brandeis got red in the face, but he nodded to Hughes and turned away.

''That will do for starters, to get the operation going,'' Carter said. ''The kind of men I'll need for an operation of this size, with this amount of notice, wouldn't walk across the street for that. Also, equipment will take a third of that amount.''

Each of the men looked at each other, and John Starkey

spoke. "Nick, the President has okayed this on the condition that France—and the rest of the world that is interested—buy it as a robbery only."

Carter understood. He rubbed his temples for a few seconds, and then looked through his fingers at Hawk. "The crew gets paid with the loot from the robbery."

Hawk shrugged. "That's about it. No one outside this room knows anything."

Carter sighed and stood. "Hughes, put not one-fifty but *two* hundred thousand in two bags. Half is to get the men interested, half is for equipment."

Hughes turned to Brandeis. The man got a little redder, and nodded.

"Where?" Hughes asked.

"The train station in Munich, a locker. Leave the key in an envelope with my name on it with Herr Carl Lugermann at a dive called Die Rosa Geächtete. He's the owner."

Hughes chuckled. "The Pink Outlaw. That's apropos."

"I have a weird sense of humor."

"It will be there."

Carter turned to Hawk. "I'll also need—"

Hawk placed a thin briefcase on the table. "You've got it, the complete Interpol file on every major thief in the world."

Carter shook his head. What great efficiency. It would be a bitch for the next two weeks to operate without it.

Carter spent the night in the Lausanne pension, and drove back to Geneva early the next morning. Just as he had left, he reentered by the laundry room. One tired old woman gave him a disapproving glance but said nothing.

In his room, he went to work on the computer printouts from Interpol, and the interior and exterior plans of the Château Charmont.

By midmorning he had the skeleton of a good plan and the nucleus of a crew mapped out. It would be difficult to pull the whole thing off with a dark curtain over it, but it could be done.

The files from Interpol were complete, down to personal habits of each person and the names of friends and those they had worked with in the past. Carter picked five, and three alternates. These he tore off and kept together. The rest of the printouts he burned and flushed into the sewer system of Geneva.

All papers, both professional and personal, he removed from his wallet and clothing. He was putting all this in a manila envelope when there was the sound of a key in the door.

It was the bellboy with lunch.

"Ah, you're back, monsieur."

"Fit as a fiddle," Carter said and smiled. "Anyone nosy?"

"No one that I saw."

"You did well."

"*Merci*." The young man grinned sheepishly. "I also *ate* well, thanks to you."

"One more favor . . ."

"Anything, monsieur."

"My bag is packed, there. Do you have a car?"

"*Oui*, a white Seat. It is in the hotel parking area."

"Take my bag with you and put it on the front floorboard of your car. Don't worry, I'll pay my bill."

He shrugged and picked up the bag. "It means nothing to me."

Another American twenty sent him on his happy way. Carter devoured the lunch and addressed the envelope to the American embassy in Geneva, to the attention of Hawk's code name, D. F. Pause. It would find its way via diplomatic pouch to Dupont Circle in Washington, D.C.

In the lobby, he mailed the envelope and approached the desk. "I'll be leaving early in the morning for Berlin. I would like to settle my bill now."

"Of course, Monsieur Coldeck, a few moments."

With typical Swiss efficiency, it was only four moments and Carter was on the street. He walked a nine-block circle away and then back to the hotel parking lot to pick up his bag.

A taxi got him to the station in time to make two calls before the train departed for Munich.

"Hello. You said to call again. I'm calling."

"Where are you?"

"Never mind. What's important is, I have a whole new expense account."

Lola was ready with a laugh. "Darling, I love the sound of your voice. How large is your expense account?"

"Twenty-five thousand American, for starters. You interested?"

"Need you ask?" she hooted.

"I thought so," Carter chuckled. "Pack, you're going to Madrid."

"When?"

"First thing in the morning. Now, here's what I want you to do, and why . . ."

The second call was to Fräulein Ilse Mott at the Hotel Brennan in Munich.

"Fräulein Mott, I believe you are a friend of Gabin Fullmer?"

"Who wants to know?"

"My name is Grottman, Rolf Grottman. Herr Fullmer and I have never met, but he will know my name."

"Go on."

"I have a business proposition I am sure Herr Fullmer will be very interested in."

"What kind of business?"

"I will tell him that in person, at Die Rosa Geächtete, tonight at eleven sharp."

"He will get the message."

"*Danke*."

Carter hung up and ran for his train.

ELEVEN

Every big city in the world has a place like the Pink
Outlaw. They sit in sections where the elegance has long
since washed away. In the harsh, bright light of day they
are ugly and without color. Inside, they are upholstered
sewers.

But at night, with darkness softening the neighborhood
and shadows hiding the outside grime, with muted lighting
glorifying the drabness inside, places like Die Rosa
Geächtete come alive.

Carter found a table near the door and ordered a beer. A
four-piece band played American jazz, and since it was
midnight the prices had just gone up a hundred percent.
This was to pay off the police for staying open late.

The Killmaster was halfway through the beer when Gabin
Fullmer entered. He went directly to the bar, ordered, and
looked the room over with a calculated eye.

He was well over six feet and thickset, with blond, close-
cropped hair cut so short he looked nearly bald. Fifty years
earlier he could have been on a Hitler Youth poster.

Carter caught his eye. Fullmer picked up his drink and

crossed the room. Just in front of Carter, he stopped with a curt bow.

"Gabin Fullmer."

"I know," Carter said. "Sit down."

"You are Grottman?"

"I am. Sit down."

He sat, and Carter ordered another round. Waiting for it, he scanned the room to see if anyone was overly interested in them.

"Herr Grottman, I am a busy man."

Carter ignored him. He sipped his beer and watched a prostitute work on a fat tourist at the bar. Only when the drinks came and the waiter left did Carter turn to him.

"You are not busy, Fullmer. Since you went legit three years ago, you have failed twice in business. At present, you are in hock up to your ass because of those failed businesses and your extraordinary love of gambling."

"Herr Grottman . . ." He started to stand.

"It's Rolf. Sit down and listen. It might be profitable for you."

The other man got red in the face and his neck got stiffer. His hands began to tremble, so he put them in his lap. Carter could see he was fighting for control, and was pleased when he got it.

"Just what do you have in mind . . . Rolf?"

"I assume you know who I am?"

He nodded. "I asked a few questions. Aren't you supposed to be occupied in Spain?"

"I was. Ask a few more questions after you leave here. You'll find out I spent a great deal of money in the right places."

Fullmer smiled wearily. "In certain areas it helps to have a great deal of money."

"I'm sure, Gabin, that you could use an advance of

twenty-five thousand American against, perhaps, four times that much.''

Carter leaned back and let him digest this. The fat tourist at the bar had opened the prostitute's blouse and was slobbering over her bare breasts.

''Just what would this entail?'' Fullmer asked, trying to keep the excitement out of his voice, but failing.

''Later. Do you still have your contacts from the old days?''

Fullmer hesitated. ''That would depend on your needs.''

Carter took a piece of paper from his jacket and slid it across the table. ''Those are the basics. I will also need three vehicles, a van, and two small cars. All three of them must be worked over so they can outrun anything in southern France.''

''How much time would I have?''

''I want everything in Nîmes by the eighth of this month.''

''Today is the second. That's five working days. It can be done, but it would be expensive.''

''Money is no object.''

''Then I can do it. But I want a guarantee.''

''No guarantees,'' Carter growled. ''An advance of twenty-five and a full share in the outcome.''

''Which is?''

''A lot, but I don't know how much for sure.''

Fullmer's mood changed. He leaned back in the chair with a smirk on his face. ''You're just out of prison. You've got a job planned, and you've got a deadline. I think, Herr Grottman, that you need me more than I need you.''

Carter stood and dropped a couple of bills on the table. ''Fuck you, Herr Fullmer.'' He grabbed the list from the other man's hand and threaded his way through the club and outside into the chilly night air.

He was halfway down the block when he heard Fullmer's

quick footsteps. The corner was just ahead. Carter quickened his pace and turned the corner, flattening himself against the wall.

He would teach Gabin Fullmer not to play hard to get.

He came around the corner too fast and tried to slide to a stop when he saw Carter. The Killmaster stepped in quickly and gut-punched him. As he doubled over, Carter caught him with a right-hand chop on the neck.

Fullmer went down on his hands and knees and tried to swing at Carter's groin. Carter stepped back and kicked him in the chest, slamming him back against the wall. He was on top of the German before he stopped moving, his thumbs on his Adam's apple.

"Just what the hell did you figure to accomplish?" he hissed.

"Nothing," Fullmer groaned, trying to smile through the pain. "I wanted to apologize, I swear. I need the work."

Carter believed him. He let him go and pulled him to his feet. "Let's go back inside where it's warm."

As Fullmer brushed off his jacket, he glanced at Carter. "Rolf, you have a bitch of a temper."

Carter chuckled. "That's just the edge of it, my friend."

Back in the club, they ordered brandies. Fullmer massaged his chest and neck as he listened to instructions.

"This is big. There's a party, a masquerade party, near Arles on the thirteenth of the month. There should be jewels on top of jewels, dollars, pounds, and francs lying around for the taking. It's hard to say just how big."

Fullmer's pain went away. "How many splits?"

"Other than myself, five."

His smile got broader. "Give me the rest of it. I'll be in Nîmes with everything on the eighth."

"Everyone goes into Spain legal. We train there. We come back over the frontier at night so there's no exit stamp on our passports. That will be on the eleventh. We set up on the twelfth, and go the next night.''

''And make for Spain as though we've been there all the time?''

''Exactly,'' Carter said, nodding.

''I'm in, all the way. What happens now?''

''Meet me at the Hauptbahnhof in two hours, entrance Two, off the Bayer Strasse. Be ready to go.''

Fullmer stood. ''Sorry about before.''

Carter smiled. ''You'll be even sorrier if it happens again.'' He waited until the other man had been gone for five minutes, then summoned his waiter.

''Ja, mein Herr?''

''Is Herr Lugermann in the club?''

''I don't know,'' the man said evasively. ''Perhaps I can help you.''

''Tell Carl that Nick is out here and wants to talk to him. But I don't want to be obvious about it. I'd like to handle it so that no one knows I'm going to see him. I'll do whatever he suggests.''

''I'll see,'' the waiter said, and slipped away.

Carter listened to the combo and waited. They were good. They finished one number and were starting on another when the waiter returned. He was carrying a fresh drink.

''Sorry,'' he said, his voice low as he picked up Carter's empty glass. ''I have instructions to spill this drink on you and to tell you to make a scene when it happens.''

''All right.'' Carter got out a cigarette and started to light it.

The waiter set the drink down and started to turn away. As he did, his tray hit the glass. It and the emptied glass both landed in Carter's lap.

''What the hell's the matter with you?'' Carter said loudly. ''Drunk or something? Look at my suit!''

"I'm so sorry, mein Herr," the waiter murmured. He was mopping at Carter's pants with a napkin.

"To hell with being sorry! What about my suit?"

The waiter glanced around nervously as though he were worried about the other customers witnessing this scene. He gave up trying to blot Carter's suit and straightened up.

"If you'll just follow me, mein Herr, everything will be taken care of."

"It had better be," Carter snarled as he followed.

The waiter turned and headed toward the rear of the room. They went all the way to the back, then turned into a little corridor. There were several doors opening off it. He stopped at the first one.

"In there," he whispered.

"Thanks," Carter said.

He opened the door and stepped inside. Carl Lugermann was sitting behind a desk covered with papers. He was a big man with dark hair, now beginning to thin. Otherwise he looked about the same as the last time Carter had seen him.

He looked up as Carter closed the door and a smile spread over his face. "Nick," he said. "It's good to see you. How'd you like the service?"

"Very inventive, as usual," Carter said with a grin, crossing the room and shaking hands.

The big man dropped back into his seat and pulled open a drawer. "You move fast. That only came a couple of hours ago." He slid an envelope across the desk.

Carter put the envelope in his pocket. "Are you still flying, Carl?"

"Sure."

"Still park your plane at Orlfurg?"

"That's right," the man replied, and smiled. "You got something on your tail?"

"I don't think so, but I want to make sure."

"Where to?"

"Milan. It's worth five big ones, American."

The big German hooted. "For that, I'll carry you over piggyback! When?"

"About three hours."

"I'll be gassed and ready." Lugermann stood and moved to the far wall. Pressing a concealed button, he slid a book-case open into the room. Behind it was a long, lighted corridor. "This goes out through the basement."

Carter saluted him and headed down the corridor.

At the number Two entrance of the train station, Carter spotted Fullmer and shook his head slightly. The man stayed where he was behind his newspaper, and Carter walked to the large room lined with lockers.

The key fit locker 527. Inside were two medium-sized valises. Carter hauled them out and went to the men's room. In one of the far rear stalls, he transferred twenty thousand from one to the other.

At the washbasins, he set both bags on his right side and began to splash water on his face. In the mirror he checked the three other occupants, one in a stall, one drying his hands, and one just leaving.

Fullmer came in, used the urinal, and moved to a basin two down from Carter.

"Bag on your side," Carter whispered out of the side of his mouth.

"Okay."

"Eighty big ones. The first twenty-five is yours."

"That should more than do it."

"I hope you know how to move it as well as spend it."

"I do."

Carter picked up the closest bag. As he passed Fullmer, the man spoke a last time.

"You trust me with all that on such short acquaintance?"

"Don't have any reason not to. Only one man ever crossed

me so far . . . Klaus Gaubman.''

Carter smiled to himself as he pushed through the swinging doors into the waiting room. Klaus Gaubman was a small-time doper who had been found mutilated in an alley a year earlier. Carter didn't know who'd killed him, but he was pretty sure Fullmer wouldn't know either.

There were five trains leaving for various points in the next hour. Three of them were heading west and would pass through the village of Orlfurg. Carter bought a ticket on each of the westbound trains in intervals from three different agents. All three tickets were for a first-class private compartment. Then he bought a newspaper and found a bench directly in the center of the waiting room.

The first train was gone and there were five minutes until the second, when two men rushed into the waiting room and did a quick imitation of nonchalant boredom when they spotted him. They split at once, each of them heading for the two entrances to the tracks.

Carter couldn't be sure, but he thought he remembered the smaller of the two. He was dressed in a heavy brown overcoat, a white woolen scarf, and a fur hat. There had been a man dressed just like him in the lobby of the Geneva hotel when Carter had paid his bill.

If the two men were one and the same, the Berlin ploy hadn't worked.

The second westbound train was just pulling out when Carter rushed to the platform. White Scarf was right behind him and the other man was running for a phone.

Carter swung aboard, knowing that White Scarf was doing the same. He found his sleeping compartment and waited for the conductor to pass through. When his ticket was punched, Carter locked the door and sauntered to the bar car.

The train rocked along lazily as he sipped a beer. There were two short stops before Orlfurg. After the second, he returned to his compartment. White Scarf wasn't around, but Carter knew he was being watched.

He waited, timing the train's progress by his watch. It was exactly eleven minutes after leaving the bar car when he felt the train losing speed on a gradient. He used a shoulder strap to keep the bag tight to his body, and lowered the window.

The train had slowed down considerably. The gradient was so sharp he could even note its steepness in the carriage. The rhythmic *clickety-click* was loud and slow, but the darkness outside seemed to be hissing past at enormous velocity.

He sensed the gradient flattening out and felt the train begin to speed up. He had to make a split-second decision. And because there might not be another opportunity to jump, he swung his legs out over the window.

He hung with his arms and head inside the compartment while he scraped with his toes to find a foothold. The slipstream tore at him, clawing him loose from his precarious hold. Telegraph poles whooshed perilously close.

Then he released. The slipstream tugged at him, suspending him as the rest of the train rolled on. He hit a grassy slope and rolled head over heels, reaching the bottom before he stopped.

He lay for a full five minutes until, in the distance, he heard the train stop at Orlfurg. Only then did he stand and get his bearings.

When he was sure of his directions, he set off at a jog. If memory served him right, it was about two miles to the small airfield where Carl Lugermann would be waiting.

"Comrade Colonel . . ."

"Yes, yes, what is it?"

Boris Arksanov dropped his briefcase on the desk and went directly to the corner of his office where a small samovar announced with a hiss that tea was made. Arksanov found it extremely difficult to function correctly without his morning tea.

"The agent, Carter, is like an eel. Our people lost him in Geneva. It was only a stroke of luck that he was spotted arriving in Munich by train."

Arksanov smiled and sipped the scalding tea. "I expected the Americans to send their best. We watch airports, he takes trains. From now on watch everything, even buses and car rental agencies."

"Yes, Comrade Colonel."

"Was he trailed in Munich?"

"Yes, and the report is he didn't spot the team."

"Well," Arksanov said dryly, "that is probably a first. Go on."

"He made contact. A man called Gabin Fullmer. He's a known criminal, a thief with a specialty as a procurer of arms. Research is trying to find more on him."

"Hmm, a thief . . . interesting. What do you suppose they are up to . . . where is he now?"

The aide coughed and grew slightly red in the face. "They lost him. Evidently he jumped from the train after leaving Munich."

Arksanov sighed wearily, as if he'd been expecting the answer. "Keep everyone on twenty-four-hour alert. He will surface again, somewhere."

"Yes, Comrade Colonel."

The aide bustled from the office and Arksanov moved to the window. Silently he sipped his tea and watched Paris come alive to a new day.

A thief, he mused. Were the Americans so stupid that they would send a common criminal to breach the army of security around René Charmont?

No, I think not.

TWELVE

As he had done every Friday evening for the last year, Regis Caylin entered Madrid's Chamartin Station and boarded the 8:10 express to San Sebastián. Caylin would have preferred to fly, but airplanes were too conspicuous, and in these troubled times air travelers were often searched.

He could ill afford being searched, going or coming. Usually, on the outbound leg, he was carrying a large amount of cash. On the return leg, he was liable to be carrying anything from stolen diamonds and securities to dope.

Regis Caylin was a smuggler. He bought low on the French side of the Pyrenees, and sold high in Madrid. When his purchases were too large for his person or briefcase— such as arms and explosives—they were trucked across the frontier and stored at a small farm he owned near Burguete. There they would be kept until a proper buyer could be found.

Caylin hadn't always been a fence and smuggler. At one time he had been a master thief himself. Some of the finest flats in the Belgravia section of his native London had been burgled by Caylin.

But eventually London had proved too warm for him. He

had left one step ahead of Scotland Yard and settled first in Morocco, and then Spain.

Now others did the thieving and he distributed the spoils. The change in occupations and climate had made Regis Caylin quite comfortable financially. And very bored.

He deposited his bag as the train pulled out, and went forward toward the dining car. A party had already started in the bar car. It was filled with tourists, mostly British and American. The men were all handsome, young, and charming, and the women were attractive and having a good time.

Caylin pushed himself through the crowd. He was almost to the door, when he found himself smack up against a tall, stunning brunette with a figure that would draw any man's eyes.

He had nearly spilled her drink in the collison. "Terribly sorry, bit of a crush."

"You're a Londoner!" she exclaimed in a slurred voice.

"I used to be. If you'll excuse me . . ."

"Wait up, darlin'! You look a little old fer me, but you're cute and you're a Londoner. So am I. Have a drink!"

He was tempted. Her body did wonderful things to a slim skirt and a tight-fitting cashmere sweater. The way her full lips pouted made her look like a playful kitten ready to romp and behave mischievously.

"Sorry." He tried to push past her.

"What's your hurry? It's a long night before San Sebastián." She wrinkled her eyes and took a deep breath.

"Busy at the moment, luv." He tried to squeeze past her again.

"How can you be busy on holiday?" she persisted.

Suddenly someone jostled her and they came together. Caylin could feel her thighs against his and her breasts pillow across his chest.

"It happens," he said. "But I'll take a raincheck."

"Well, darling, if that's the way you want it."

Her eyes drifted away, interest gone. The crowd parted and he moved on into the dining car.

He had an excellent meal and spent a leisurely hour over coffee and brandy before he paid his bill.

Weaving his way back through the party in the bar car, he tried to spot the tall, willing brunette.

She was nowhere to be seen.

He was nearly to his compartment when he saw her. She was backing out of the compartment beside his, making excuses that she was "a little tired, but maybe later."

She looked even more voluptuous and more appealing.

When the door was closed, he slipped up behind her and put an arm around her waist. She twisted her body slowly, without moving her feet, and drunkenly fell limp into his arms.

"Well, well, if it ain't you, darling," she said, lacing her fingers around his neck.

"About that drink . . ." Caylin said.

"Come along, darling," she cooed with a smile, showing small, even white teeth. "Ummmm, yes, you come along with me, darling. You might not be too old for me at that. And you are so very cute."

She took him by the hand and threaded her way down the companionway to another compartment.

"Here is where you get your drink, darling," she purred.

She unlocked the door and moved into the compartment. Caylin followed her and kicked the door closed. Just as he reached for her, she stepped back and placed her palms flat on his chest.

"Not so fast, Mr. Caylin, let's talk a little."

He was immediately on the alert. There was a sharpness in her eyes now, and suddenly she was no more drunk than he was.

"How do you know my name?"

"Oh, I know a lot about you, Regis. I know Scotland Yard would love to have you by the thumbs. I know you have a nice little place near the French frontier, where you often store unmentionables. And I know you know ways through the Pyrenees that only the goats use."

He reached for the handle. "I don't know what the hell—"

"Don't go, Regis. Sit down, let's talk. My name is Lola, and have I got a deal for you."

The flat was on North Paolo, near the Poldi-Pezzoli Museum. It was two rooms, cheap, and furnished with what could be picked up off the street. The landlady was greedy. She rented it by the month, the week, or even by the hour, when one of the whores from the Piazza della Scala caught a mark who could afford it.

It was perfect for Carter's needs.

He sat in darkness behind a table. On the table was a powerful, single-bulb lamp. The lamp was trained into the eyes of the two men occupying chairs on the other side of the table.

The two men were enough alike to be twins. They were both about six feet, well built, with olive complexions, glossy black hair and dark eyes, and square-jawed, handsome faces.

They were the Salvati brothers, Arturo and Tommaso. They both had police records inches thick, and they had both done time in Lodourno Prison south of Rome.

They had two specialties: automobiles and guns. Emotionally they were fearless, and, once mastered, were loyal.

Mastering them was the problem.

Carter had done nothing but say "Sit" since they had entered the room. Now he studied them carefully.

They wore stained coveralls and heavy, ankle-high work shoes with the tops of discolored socks showing. Sweat-stained work caps were crumpled in their laps. They picked at the caps with grime-encrusted fingers.

Carter grinned to himself. The Salvati brothers had come down a long way from the days when they wore designer suits and drove Ferraris.

"Why is it," Carter asked, "that two such intelligent men as yourselves drive a garbage truck?"

The brothers exchanged glances and their lips curled back over white teeth. Arturo spoke. "Why is it that an upstanding citizen like yourself leaves an envelope with money and the offer of a job in our truck?"

"And when we come to meet you in good faith, you hide behind a lamp that shines in our faces?" Tommaso dug a cigarette from a beat-up pack and lit it with a wooden match.

"Because," Carter replied, "I have better employment for you, but if you should decline it, I wouldn't want you to know who made the offer."

Tommaso nodded, smoke curling into his eyes. "Being the honest men that we are, we would like better employment. We have had our eye on a little hotel in Tangier. It would make a nice place for retirement."

"Would fifty thousand American help buy your hotel?" Carter asked.

"It would help," Arturo said. "But, you see, signore, my brother and I . . . well, we have spent some time in prison."

Tommaso chimed in, "Three times in prison. And if we go in a fourth time, we will never come out. So, for fifty thousand, signore, I would not take the time to piss on your grave."

Carter laughed out loud. "And if I were to say your split

of the total take could be five times that amount?''

"For that figure, signore," Arturo chuckled, "we will provide the bodies for your graveyard."

Carter outlined his plans. He left out names and places, and explained the dangers going in.

The brothers held a conference with their eyes, and turned back to the man in the darkness.

"We are agreeable," Tommaso said. "But we do not do business with a stranger."

Carter slid the passport across the desk. Both men examined it and smiled.

"I have heard of you," Arturo said. "It will be a pleasure working with you."

Carter turned on the overhead light and started piling dollars in front of them.

"This is your advance. I'm adding enough to buy a car—a large, powerful car. It must be new, and falsely registered. Can you handle that?"

"Signore Grottman, you are in Italy. You have money. Anything can be handled.

"I want you to meet me tomorrow evening in Monaco, the casino, at eight sharp. And, gentlemen, buy some clothes, good ones. You are now the driver and bodyguard of a very rich man."

Carter pulled on his coat, snapped his valise, and paused at the door.

"Wait five minutes after I leave. Then shut the lights off and leave yourselves."

In the street, he walked toward the museum. There were cabs parked all along the Corso Briera. He bypassed the first three because their drivers looked old, tired, and staid.

In the fourth he spotted a cocky young man who looked as if, for the right price, he would put wings on his cab and go to the moon. He opened the front door and slid into the passenger seat.

"You are availabe, friend?"

"*Sì, signore,*" the youth said, reaching for the flag.

Carter caught his hand. "I don't think you want to do that. Figure a price to San Remo."

The young man's eyes grew wide. "San Remo, signore? The San Remo that is on the French frontier?"

"That San Remo," Carter said, nodding. "You can't take this cab across the frontier, can you?"

"No."

"But in San Remo, I can hire a cab that can cross to Monaco?"

"*Sì, signore.*"

"Then go to San Remo."

Ten minutes outside the city, Carter crawled into the back seat and went to sleep.

The Café Lobo was in a tiny side street off the Puerto Lieta, a few blocks from the Plaza de Toros in Madrid. It was a place that tourists rarely found, a café where *toreros* and members of their *cuadrilla* went when they wanted privacy. It was also fancied by *banderilleros* and *picadores* who did not frequent the more well-known cafés when they were looking for work.

It was here that Lola went in search of Carter's fifth man. Years before, during her "Serena" period, she had spent many profitable nights in the Café Lobo.

Old Mama Cadiz remembered her, and came bounding out of the kitchen when her arrival was announced.

"Serena, my little chick!" the old woman exclaimed, clamping the younger woman to her ample bosom. "You are more beautiful than ever! How many men have you ruined since I last saw you?"

"More than I can count, Mama, more than I can count,"
Lola answered, smiling.

The two women migrated to a private table in the depths
of the café and, over glasses of brandy, Lola explained her
needs.

When she finished, Mama Cadiz smiled shrewdly. "Ah,
Serena, the larceny in your heart. When will you find a
good man and settle down?"

"There are no good men, Mama, and I will settle down
when I am old and rich. Can you help me?"

"There is such a young man as you describe. He is a
novillero from Sevilla. He is good, but not good enough
for Madrid."

"Then a sum of money such as this would interest him?"

"I think so, yes. I have heard that in the ring he is all
heart and no wrists. You know the rewards of that."

Lola nodded. "The horn."

"His name is Paco Torres. But there is a problem . . . ."

"Oh?"

"He is spending now a little time in jail. It is said that,
being unable to purchase swords of his own, he appropriated
several belonging to someone else."

Lola smiled. "Then he should be very receptive. Where?"

"Toledo."

"Your commission, Mama, will be in next week's mail."
Lola hurried out to her rented car.

Paco Torres was darkly handsome, tall and lean, with the
narrow hips, the chiseled jaw, and the cynical bearing of
the matador he would never become.

As Lola watched him strut toward her, she knew he would
be perfect.

"You are my benefactor, señorita?"

"I am, and seeing you makes me wonder why. You look like a stable boy. Have you other clothes?"

His eyes went down to the threadbare black pants, crumpled and dirty, the worn shoes, and the sweaty shirt. He felt his face, and the stubble was stiff enough to scratch his palm.

He looked back up at her and smiled with a good-natured shrug. "Once a peasant, always a peasant."

"Let us hope not. Come along."

The sun was bright, and walking beside this beautiful, voluptuous woman gave Torres a good feeling, a feeling that his rotten luck was about to change.

She used a perfume that was not too strong, and he could smell it as they walked, just enough to reach his nostrils and make him want to smell more deeply of it. The top of her head was on a level with his mouth, and he looked down at her, at the point of the V made by the neckline of her dress.

She looked at him. "And does it please the young matador?"

He ignored her mockery, letting his eyes meet hers. "If it was meant to be hidden," he said, "then I have wronged you."

She laughed. "Wronged me! I have been stared at before and by better than you."

He shook his head. "Not by better," he said.

"Richer, then."

"Richer, yes."

Lola opened her purse and pulled out several bills. "Do you have a passport?"

"*Sí*. I worked once in the *caudrilla* of Tobalo and had to travel to Mexico."

"Good. Here, get a shave and buy yourself some decent

clothes and shoes. Meet me in an hour there, at that café.''

He paused. ''May I ask where we go from there, señorita?''

''To Madrid, and then to France and Monaco.''

His teeth flashed in his dark face. ''Am I to be your stud, or something else?''

''Something else,'' she replied, ''if you're a good boy.''

THIRTEEN

The garage of Pierre Sobrene was in the hill country of Monts de Vaucluse east of Avignon. It was a shabby place, the meanest in a warren of mean buildings. From the nearby road it looked like an endless maze of structures strung together with no purpose.

Only Sobrene himself knew the purpose of all the buildings. The interior walls of wood or brick looked as if they had been there for a long time. Actually, each and every one of them was movable. A vehicle could disappear into one building and come out another, with a new color, a different engine, and a whole new set of chassis numbers.

Two cars were currently going through this process under the watchful eyes of Gabin Fullmer and Pierre Sobrene.

Sobrene was a square-faced, thin-lipped little man with hooded eyes and tobacco-stained teeth. He combed his hair straight back without a part and wore it long on the back of his neck.

He looked more like a Paris *mec* who ran girls than a mechanic.

"Will they be ready day after tomorrow?" Fullmer asked.

"The suspension you'll need for those kinds of speeds on mountain roads will be tricky, but they'll be ready."

131

"And the engines?"

Sobrene cackled. "For the kind of money you're paying me, monsieur, you could run these two in Formula One at Monte Carlo."

"Good," Fullmer said. "I will check with you tomorrow."

He left the garage and drove one of Sobrene's cars into Avignon. At the hotel, he approached the switchboard operator.

"I would like to send a wire to Monaco, please."

"The agent, Carter, is like a ghost, Comrade Colonel, but following the woman from London has paid dividends."

"You have lost Carter?" Boris Arksanov hissed.

"I am afraid so, completely."

The Paris *rezident* sighed. "Then tell me what you have on the others."

"The woman made contact with a man named Regis Caylin on a train from Madrid to San Sebastián. She immediately took another train back to Madrid."

"And this Caylin?" Arksanov asked.

He listened patiently, sipping his vodka and asking pointed questions as his aide relayed the meeting on the train between the woman and Regis Caylin. He explained the report of the theft of two automobiles by Fullmer, and their present whereabouts. They also had a fair account of Gabin Fullmer's purchases.

By the end of the report, Arksanov was smiling and nodding.

"Thieves! This Carter is recruiting a band of professional thieves!"

"It would seem so."

"Then we have it, and a good plan it is."

"You think they are going to rob Charmont?"

"Of course. They will stage it as though a group of

thieves hold up a wealthy gathering. You say this Caylin has a place just over the frontier?"

"Yes, Comrade Colonel," the aide replied, spreading a map of northern Spain on the desk. "It is here in the mountains north of Burguete. Supposedly it is a ranch for the raising of bulls, but actually it is used to store contraband until it can be sold and moved on."

"How many men can we mass there?"

The aide shrugged. "As many as needed."

"Then do it. Take over the ranch, and have our Basque friends watch every trail in from France. We will have two tries at them . . . one on the mountain, and, if they get through, one at the ranch."

"I will make the arrangements, Comrade Colonel."

The aide left and Arksanov refilled his glass.

Neat, very neat, he thought. And that pig René Charmont could go to hell for his ten million.

Paco Torres closed the door behind him and stood without moving, blinking into the glare of the floodlamps. The light was a blazing curtain around him. He could see nothing of the room but the stark outline of a chair placed so that, no matter which direction its occupant faced, it would be looking directly into at least one floodlamp.

"Your name is Paco Torres."

He tugged at the lapels of his new jacket. "Yes."

"Sit down. You'll have to excuse the lights. They are for your protection as well as mine. I have a proposition for you. If you should decide not to take it, it is better you never know who made the offer."

Torres sat, feeling the sweat gather in the small of his back and in his crotch.

"There is a table by your chair with sunglasses, if the light hurts your eyes."

"I am used to the glare. It is like the sun over the *plaza de toros* on a hot Sunday afternoon.''

Carter appraised him from the darkness. He had the size, the bearing, and the dark good looks. Only a close intimate would know the difference.

"Paco, the job we have planned pays twenty-five thousand dollars flat. You'll be the inside man, with certain things to do just before we go. When the job goes down, you become a spectator. That's it. Interested?''

Torres smiled wide, his white teeth gleaming in his dark face. "I think I'm going to enjoy Mexico.''

Carter pushed a Spanish magazine across the table. "Here's how you get in.''

The magazine was open to a picture of a matador and a charging bull. The matador was just finishing a move with his cape, with his face in profile.

It was all clear to Torres now. He nodded and smiled again. "It is Manolo the Tiger. In the provincial cafés I am often mistaken for him by young girls.''

"That's why you're here,'' Carter said. "One thing, Paco. No women. From now on until it's over, you stay zipped up. I don't want you shot by a jealous husband and ruin the whole setup. Got it?''

"*Sí*. From now on until Mexico, Paco Torres is a saint.''

Carter turned the light on and the Salvati brothers came forward to shake Torres's hand.

"Arturo, Tommaso, fill him in. We'll all leave in the morning in the Bentley.''

Carter left the room and walked around Monaco harbor past the casino to the Hotel de Paris.

There was a message in his box: *All the special toys are present and accounted for. Presently in the Alban, Avignon. Gabin.*

He rode the elevator to his suite. Lola was in the sitting room in front of the television. She snapped it off when he entered.

"Will Torres do?"

"He'll be fine, if I can control him," Carter said. "He's a cocky little bastard. A wire came from Fullmer. He's all set in Avignon."

Lola stood. She wore a deep red flamenco costume, the neck cut low to expose much of her full bosom.

"You like?" she asked, twirling so the ruffled skirt whirled out around her ankles.

"You look every inch the part," Carter said. "Take it off."

"What?"

He chuckled. "I don't want to tear it."

She did, slowly, like an accomplished stripper. When it was off, lying on the floor around her feet, she added her underwear to it.

"Olé," she murmured, stretching toward the ceiling.

Carter slid his arms around her and they kissed slowly, tongues exploring, darting, joining. He pulled her to him and ran his hands over her body as hers went to work on his clothes.

She reached for the jacket he wore and undid his shirt. Without speaking she led him to the bedroom. There was nothing to say. She watched, amused, as he laid his holstered Luger down so it couldn't fall. He pulled her down and gently nibbled her breasts. Her nipples hardened as his teeth scored them. He ran his hand up the inside of her thigh but didn't touch her. His hand and mouth moved together until they reached her center. He held her open as her hands moved over him, stroking.

Her voice was a low moan in her throat as she called his name over and over, in passion and he tasted her. With a strangled cry she pushed him onto his back and moved over him. She sat and threw her legs back so that he was thrust fully inside her. They lay locked as she rotated her hips slowly.

She began to breathe raggedly as he gripped her by the arms and thrust up into her. She was excited by his urgency. He held her hips as they both began to breathe quickly, their bodies moving in tandem, spiraling together toward their climax.

She cried out as she felt herself contract, and the sensation forced her eyes shut for a moment. When she opened them again she saw the smile on his face and the drops of sweat on his forehead.

"When do we leave?" she asked.

"In the morning."

"There is something I have to tell you."

"Like what?"

She rolled to her side, gently keeping him trapped inside her. "Torres and I were followed from Madrid."

"On the plane?"

She nodded. "I recognized him from a long time ago."

"Oh?"

"His name is Bulgakov. At one time he was with the KGB unit in London."

"You're sure he was following you?"

"Positive. He picked up two more to make a team when we landed in Nice."

Carter lit a cigarette. "Then it's only a matter of time until they make me."

"What do we do?"

"Go right on," Carter replied, "and let them make the first move."

FOURTEEN

Gabin Fullmer, Tommaso Salvati, and Carter rode the bus from Avignon to Arles. They spent the better part of the afternoon with packs on their backs, tramping the hills photographing birds and the country scenes.

Around dusk they made their way to a high point about a mile from the Charmont château.

It sat atop a steep hill on about forty acres of lawn, and it was quite a sight to behold. The main residence was flanked by two smaller houses, quarters for the help.

The château itself was five stories tall, with a mansard roof dotted with vanes and chimney pots and covered with heavy gray slabs of slate. No other buildings were in sight, and the entire park area was surrounded by a high iron-spear fence painted black, with the tips in gilt. Beyond this formidable fence on all sides was thick forest.

As all three of them snapped pictures, they commented.

"That fence is electrified," Fullmer offered.

"And ten to one there's a warning grid in the ground inside it," Tommaso added. "See the way the walking guards stay about twenty feet inside the fence on their patrols?"

Carter nodded. "Lola will be able to take care of that. It's the television cameras that may give us a problem."

When each of them had taken a full roll of film, they set aside their cameras and brought high-powered glasses into play.

"It's good there's only one entrance besides the main one in front," Tommaso said. "If we plug that, and cover the river, no one can slip through us."

Carter spent another twenty minutes covering everything with the binoculars. Beyond the walls of the house, the fields stretched a deep green in the setting sun. On either side there were magnificent gardens, and straight ahead, below the villa, the Rhône River. A huge grillwork gate that barred the single entrance had been opened and a truck moved out slowly with a load of clippings from the garden. They had been working on those gardens all afternoon.

"The grounds staff will go home for the night. That leaves twenty household staff, give or take a couple. Gabin, have you got the guards?"

"Two on the front gates, one on the river, and two on the roof. Add the four rovers on the fence, that makes nine. Figure three shifts, that makes twenty-seven."

"Jesus," Tommaso groaned, "a bloody army."

Carter smiled. "I never said it would be easy. Gabin, what about the television and alarm monitor room?"

"Well, we've seen the shift change. My guess is the off-duty crew probably doubles in three two-man teams, three hours each."

"A good guess," Carter said. "Once we're in, we'll have to hit the main house from top to bottom at the same time, to get all the guests cornered before they catch on they're being hit."

"How many guests do you figure?" Fullmer asked.

"About a hundred and fifty."

"And how do we get on the roof?" asked Tommaso. "Fly?" He took a drink of wine and scratched his beard.

"No way to climb up there from the outside," Fullmer said, studying the château. "No way that could be depended on."

"The roof men," Carter explained, "can approach through the gardens, and use a grappling hook and rope ladder for the roof."

"How about the guests?" Tommaso asked. "We herd them all into one room?"

"Usually the gambling takes place on the third floor, with the ground and second floor given over to dancing and eating. And the bedroom floors are used by the guests for their indiscretions."

"Is that what they call it in international society?" Fullmer asked dryly.

"That's it," Carter chuckled. "The fifth floor is Charmont's private domain. That will be the toughest nut to crack. I'll explain that later."

Again he peered through the glasses.

"Two men coming down from the hill will take care of the chauffeurs, and then move on toward the main gate and take care of the guards inside the walls. River men will cut the main telephone wires"—Fullmer made a note of it— "and converge in time with the front-gate men, while roof men strip the upper floors and we meet on the third floor, or wherever the gambling rooms are."

Tommaso looked at him. "You still haven't said what we do with the guests."

"Everybody is brought into the house."

"That could prove difficult," Fullmer said.

"Get them all together," Carter replied. "That's necessary. You never know which one might be carrying the family fortune, or wearing her grandmother's precious diamond necklace.''

Carter removed the binoculars from his eyes and lit a cigarette. ''All right, Gabin, sing it back to me.''

Fullmer recited his notes. Night was falling when he finished.

''Okay. Gabin, you get back to Avignon and gather everything and everybody. You know where to plant the equipment. Make sure everybody goes over the frontier separately. Tommaso and I will meet you in Burguete tomorrow night.''

''Right.''

Carter turned to Salvati. ''Tommaso, let's go meet your man in Marseilles.''

At two in the morning much of Marseilles was quiet. The so-called ''black hole of the Mediterranean'' was still raucous near the port, but the inner city slept.

Carter and Tommaso walked from the train station through twisting alleys, often doubling back on themselves. They changed cabs three times.

''*Scusi, signore,*'' Tommaso said, ''but you are acting like a man who thinks he is being followed.''

''Cautious, Tommaso, just cautious.''

Actually, Carter had not seen a tail all day, but he couldn't shake the feeling that one was there.

On Boulevard Garibaldi, they caught a fourth cab and Tommaso gave the driver an address in the port section.

They left the main streets of the city and entered the harbor area. The streets were dark and the blank brick walls of the monotonous rows of warehouses on either side echoed to the stuttering exhaust of the cab. They rounded a corner and ahead was the weak light of an all-night café. In the

distance Carter could see the outlines of the ships riding
anchor on mooring buoys, waiting to get alongside the piers
inside the seawall.

There was no moon and it was very dark.

Carter paid the driver and they went inside. The café was
a dungeon of dirty whitewashed walls, a galvanized iron
bar, and wire tables and chairs. There were no women and
every chair was filled.

The bartender looked up from pouring a glass of wine
and gave them a flat, level appraisal. He was a tough, with
remote eyes and deliberate movements. His voice, when he
spoke to them, was tired and uninterested. *"Bon soir."*

"Hello, Pipi," Tommaso said, and waved Carter to stay
behind while he disappeared through a back door. The bartender leaned his fleshy arms on the dirty iron bar and
seemingly forgot Carter was there as he explored his right
ear with a dirty finger. A few minutes later the back door
opened and a short dark man near fifty, with a heavy, recently shaved black beard walked toward Carter, with Salvati
behind him.

"This is Porto," Tommaso said, and moved to one side.

"You are Grottman?"

"I am," Carter said, and handed the other man his
passport.

Porto Lazzoni was several inches under six feet, broad
through the chest, with sloping shoulders. His features were
blank and never changed.

He eyed the passport and handed it back to Carter. "We
can talk in the back."

They passed down a long hallway with rooms on both
sides. The end door led into a kitchen. As they passed
through it, Carter was struck with the incongruity. Unlike
everything else in the café, the kitchen itself was gleaming
white, immaculate, and equipped with the very latest in

appliances. An eight-burner stove stood along one wall, a washing machine and dryer, and at the far end, an ironer. A huge restaurant-sized refrigerator covered most of the other wall. A porcelain table was in the middle, its top spotlessly clean.

Porto walked directly to the refrigerator, opened it, and began rummaging around. They were soon settled back with a hunk of cheese and bottles of wine.

"Tommaso says you want three people to be guests on my boat for a while."

Carter nodded. "Twenty-four hours will be long enough."

"One hundred thousand francs."

"Sixty," Carter countered, chewing the cheese.

"Eighty."

"Seventy."

Porto seemed to think for a moment, and then shouted, "Julio!"

The door opened and a young man of about twenty-five stepped inside. He was tall and thin with delicate bones. He leaned against the door and held the knob behind him. He stared at Carter with black, insolent eyes.

"This is my partner, Julio," Porto said. "What do you think, Julio?"

"Three, you say?"

Carter nodded. "A driver and a man and a woman."

"Any chance we may have to kill them?"

"Not unless you fuck up and let them see your faces."

The two partners exchanged looks and nodded. "Seventy-five," Porto announced, "and we will feed them while they are in our care."

"Done," Carter said. From his valise he counted out seventy-five thousand francs. He then spread out a map.

Julio pushed away from the door and walked softly toward

Carter. He stood very close, leaning one hand on the table, the other close to a knife at his belt.

"You carry much money, signore. What is to stop us from just taking all your money and dropping you in the harbor? It is done often."

Carter matched his smile. "You want to try it?"

The tension lasted a full minute before Porto reached for the wine bottle and spoke. "Come, come, we are businessmen here. Julio, sit down. Don't be greedy."

Reluctantly Julio took the fourth seat at the table and Carter leaned over the map.

"They will be coming over from Spain on the morning of the thirteenth, a Saturday. It will probably be midmorning, but you'd better be out early watching for them."

"Where?" Porto asked.

"At Port-Bou, here. You'll have to take them before they reach Perpignan. How and where is up to you. They will be in a gray Rolls-Royce. The license number is here in the margin of the map. Burn the map when you're set."

Porto and Julio studied the map. "We can bring them aboard here, south of Canet-Plage," Julio said.

Porto nodded. "And Marcus can hide the Rolls until we release them."

They both looked up at Carter and nodded.

"This number is for a highway call box just outside Marseilles. Call just as soon as you have them."

"Just one thing, signore," Julio said. "Who are these people?"

"The matador Manolo, his mistress, and their driver."

"Damn," Julio hissed, "it should be worth more money!"

Carter smiled and counted out another twenty-five thousand francs. "It is. Let's go, Tommaso."

• • •

Carter and Tommaso bused from Marseilles to Perpignon and took the train across the border and down to Barcelona. There, Carter made reservations for them on three flights and purchased tickets. The flights were to Madrid, Malaga, and Pamplona, and they all left at approximately the same time.

When, at the last moment, they ran for the Pamplona flight, Carter spotted the man spotting them.

René Charmont was rich and powerful, but he didn't have an organization so big that he could cover every airport in Europe.

No, Carter thought, an organization far bigger than Charmont's was tracking his progress. And he was pretty sure he knew who it was.

At Pamplona, they hired a car and a driver. It was dark by the time they drove north toward Burguete and the Pyrenees. The moon rose, large and bright, and the countryside slipped by, bright silver mingled with black and silent shadows. Hills rose up against the sky, not sharp, but rounded like a woman's body, thrusting up gently from the earth. It grew cold and no lights showed as the car sped along and only rarely did they pass another vehicle.

There were no lights following them. This told Carter that even though their arrival in Pamplona had been noted, there was no attempt to follow them further.

That meant that his watchers already knew where he was going.

It was well after midnight when they arrived, pulling off the road onto a bumpy and narrow dirt path that led twistingly, between tall trees, to a massive stone house high on a hillside. A hound barked somewhere behind the house and was answered by another.

Stiff, Carter climbed from the car, looking around at the

darkness. A light gleamed faintly through a deep-set window that was more like an embrasure in a fort. A heavy wooden door, massive, like the house, was pushed open and two people emerged, Lola and their host, Regis Caylin.

Carter paid, dismissed the car, and mounted the steps with Tommaso close behind. Lola introduced them to Caylin and they entered the huge old house.

Carter could see that the walls were almost two feet thick and that the door was covered with elaborate ironwork that must have dated back hundreds of years. Everything about the house at once impressed him with its age and its sense of permanence. Its very massiveness gave it the feeling of being rooted in the soil on which it stood, immovable, belonging there as much as the hills themselves. Inside, the ceiling was high, very high, with huge ancient wooden beams thrust across it. To his right he could see the flickering light of a wood fire and he went directly to it.

Everyone else was there, all gathered around a large table piled with cold meats, cheeses, and wine.

Carter looked around the room. This was the first time they had all been together. They looked at him expectantly, and he knew that now was the time to spell out his complete authority.

"From this moment on, everything I say is gospel. I give an order, you take it, no questions asked. First thing in the morning, we'll unpack the gear and start to train."

"Train?" Arturo Salvati cried. "You mean, like soldiers?"

"Close. For tonight, Gabin, break out the walkie-talkies. Make sure everyone knows how they work. Carry them with you all the time. Caylin, since you know the place, you stand first watch. Everybody stands guard, four on, twenty off. Where's a good place?"

"The top floor of the grain building would make a perfect

spot. It's high and you can see everything.''

"Good. Grab a walkie and get going. The rest of you get some sleep. You're going to need it.''

One by one they moved off. Lola came close to Carter. "We have the first-floor bedroom in the rear.''

"Go ahead and turn in. I'm going to have a look around outside.''

Outside, it was crisp and getting colder. Carter stood until he could make out the objects in the yard before walking toward the grain building. Suddenly he stood stock-still, his senses on full alert.

He thought he had heard it when he stepped outside, but it wasn't until he got his foot on the step that he knew. A car, possibly on the main road. He hurried up the stairs to find Caylin crouched before one of the peepholes in the wood-battened windows.

"Is it turning into our road?'' Carter asked.

"Gone on past.'' Caylin shook his head.

"Did it stop at all . . . or even slow down?''

"I don't think so. It was going pretty steady.''

"Someone could have jumped from a moving car,'' Carter growled, straining his eyes in the darkness. "Better be careful . . . and warn Arturo when he relieves you.''

Caylin straightened up. "Who knows we're here?''

"Let's hope nobody,'' Carter replied, knowing it wasn't true. "Lola will take the first watch in the morning after Arturo.''

"Right.''

Carter started for the stairs, then stopped, turning to face the other man. "Caylin, I'm curious about something. What made you agree to this? I hear you're loaded.''

The other man smiled. "I am. But I'm also bored.''

Shaking his head, Carter descended the stairs and returned to the main house. The bedroom was bathed in moonlight.

He partially closed the drapes and undressed. Lola moved close to him when he crawled into the bed.

"There's something wrong, isn't there," she whispered.

"Yeah," he growled. "You wouldn't be playing footsie with your old buddies from Moscow, would you?"

Her body stiffened against him. "Would you believe me if I told you no?"

"I'll believe you."

"I'm not."

"Good. I'd really hate to have to kill you after all we've come to mean to each other."

"Bastard."

"Bitch."

Silence.

"Nick . . . ?"

"Yeah."

"Remember, I know who you are and what you do."

"So?"

"All of us, including little old larcenous me, are going in there for the loot. Want to tell me what the hell you're going in for?"

"You think you really want to know?"

She took a long time to answer.

"Want to make love?"

"No," he said, "go to sleep."

She went to work with her talented hands. He managed to hold out a whole minute.

FIFTEEN

Carter had only three days to acquaint them with every aspect of the raid and drill them into an organized unit. With this crew he was pretty sure he could do it.

Immediately after breakfast the following morning, the packs that had been brought over the mountains by Fullmer, Arturo, and Caylin were unloaded.

Gabin Fullmer had done an excellent job. There were wire cutters, heavy leather gloves and skintight silk ones. Pencil flashlights with spare bulbs and batteries; several spools of medical tape, industrial tape, and four hundred feet of seven-hundred-pound test nylon rope with fourteen-inch-spread grappling hooks. There were tubes of black theatrical makeup and black Basque-type berets that could be pulled low over the forehead.

In the smaller packs there were wristwatches with sweep-second hands in large faces, black cloth to be made into handkerchief masks, flat steel jimmy tools, and tiny capsules of explosive plastique.

Most important of all, there were the short-range stun guns and sawed-off shotguns. Carter explained as he rationed out the equipment.

"Anybody uses one of the shotguns to shoot up anything but the château for fear purposes, I put a bullet of my own into. I dodn't mind the Sûreté coming after us for robbery, but murder is stupid. Anybody looks too hard to control—including the guards—use the stun guns."

He got no argument.

When black sneakers and heavy blue coveralls were passed out and everyone was suited up, he took them outside.

They started with light exercises and worked up to a long run before they broke for lunch. After eating, they set up the exterior of the grain building as the target. Then, using the grappling tools, the rope ladders, and everything that would be applicable, they went through the first phase step by step.

When it was time for the evening meal, everyone was dead tired but morale was high.

Over coffee and brandy that night, Carter doled out the particular jobs that they seemed best suited for from the day's exercises.

"Lola and Paco will already be in, posing as Manolo and his mistress. Arturo will come in via the river in the wet suit. The river guard and the perimeter guards are his responsibility. Gabin and myself will go over the fence, here, where it's dark. We'll get the two on the roof. Tommaso, when you see our signal, you wander down to the main gate and take care of the guards there. You'll already be on the grounds as Manolo's chauffeur."

"What about the electric fence, the grid, and the cameras?"

"That's Lola and Paco's job. I'll get to it. When the perimeter is secure, everyone on the grounds will get the off-duty guards. They'll be in this building. Herd them into the wine cellar. There's only one door and no windows. Once that door is locked, they are in there for the duration."

"And that's when you start herding the guests inside from the pool?" Lola asked.

"Right," Carter said, nodding. "If we're quiet and fast, they won't know anything is happening until it's too late. Everyone is shuffled to the third floor where we can watch them. Any other questions?"

"Only one," said Caylin. "How do we get out?"

"Later," Carter replied. "You'll get that the last night before we shove off. Right now you all have enough to think about. Everybody but Paco and Lola get some sleep."

The others left, and Carter laid out the interior floor plan of the château. He went over every inch of the first four floors with both of them.

"You'll plant ten charges at the places I've marked. I'll have the radio on the roof to arm the detonators when the time comes."

"How powerful are they?" Lola asked.

"More noise and smoke than anything else, but they will be a good diversion, and the way they are placed the guests will be forced to move toward the third floor. Now, Paco, this is important. The alarm system is here, in this basement room. At exactly midnight, you must be in that room. Gabin will show you what wires to cut in order to de-electrify the fence and the grid. Got that?"

"*Sì.*"

"Directly above the basement room, on the first floor, here, is the television monitoring room. Two men. You'll have only a minute to get up there after we start in. Those two men will see us on their monitors. When they realize the alarm is out, they'll bust out of that room to sound it by shouting. Your job is to stop them. Everything clear?"

"*Sì,*" the young Spaniard said, his face breaking into a leering grin. "You have said nothing about the fifth floor. Could it be that on the fifth is where the real loot is and you are saving it for yourself?''

"The fifth floor is my business, Paco. You'll get all you can spend off the third floor. You've got the eight-to-midnight watch. Move!''

Torres glared and grumbled a little, but he picked up his walkie and left. Carter poured himself a brandy.

"Nick . . .''

"Shhh," Carter said. "Rolf, remember?''

"Okay, Rolf, baby," she said, riffling through the plans on the table. "Paco's right. There's no floor plan to the fifth floor.''

"Yes, there is," Carter said, patting his breast pocket, "right here. Let's go into the bedroom. It's time you learned what's going on.''

She followed him into the bedroom, where he turned on a lamp and spread the floor plan of the fifth story out on the bed.

"The entire floor is René Charmont's inner sanctum. The small elevator in the house runs only to the fourth floor. The stairway leading up to the fifth floor is protected top and bottom by electrically operated veneer-sheathed doors. On the fifth floor itself, the doors are compartmentalized by similar steel-lined doors.''

"It's a bloody fortress!''

"The château *is* a fortress," Carter replied. "The fifth floor is a fortress *inside* a fortress. When all hell starts, my guess is that Charmont, his mistress, and one of the female guests will go like hell for the fifth floor. I want you at the bottom of those stairs waiting for them. If they get in there and shut those doors, I'll never get to them.''

Lola's eyes narrowed and she got that little catlike grin he knew so well, the one that showed her eyeteeth.

"What's on that fifth floor that you set this whole bloody caper up for?''

He told her, and added, "That's what I want. What's up there for you is a bearer certificate for ten million Swiss francs in gold. Are you in?"

"Like I say, mate, I'm yer girl. Who's the bird going up with Charmont and the mistress?"

"Bella Arksanova. She's the wife of the Paris *rezident*, and a KGB major."

"Well now, luv, that kind of explains the whole tickle, don't it?"

Carter smiled. "I love it when you talk dirty. You'd better get some sleep. You have to relieve Paco at midnight."

"Nick, Nick, wake up!"

He came awake slowly from a deep slumber. Had it been anyone but Lola he would have been alert immediately, but the second he heard her voice he fought wakefulness.

"Yeah, what is it?"

"Our boy, Paco. He got a case of the hots and took off for the village on one of the bicycles."

Carter sat up instantly. "What?"

"He made some moves on me toward the shift change. When I politely told him to go play with himself, he took off."

"All right, crawl in and get some extra sack time yourself. I'll take the rest of your watch."

"You mean you're not going after him?"

"No use," the Killmaster replied. "Whatever damage he's done is done by now."

He dressed, grabbed himself a cup of coffee from the always-going pot in the kitchen, and headed for the granary.

Tommaso arrived just before four, at the normal end of Lola's watch, and was surprised to find Carter there. The Killmaster explained, and both men settled down in gloomy silence to wait for their horny colleague.

"What will you do, Signore Rolf?"

"Teach him some manners."

"Me, I would kill him."

"Me," Carter said, "I would like to, but we need him too much."

Paco Torres rode into the compound just at first light. He dropped the bicycle carelessly and, whistling, walked toward the main house. Carter met him halfway.

"You won't learn, will you, Paco," he growled.

The young man shrugged. "I am not cut out to be a soldier. Don't worry, there was no problem."

"I'll shoot you between the eyes if you step out of line once more," Carter said with restraint, but not enough to keep his voice from quivering.

Torres's lips curled. He went for a knife at his belt. Carter chopped his wrist. The knife dropped to the ground. Carter brought up a right hand and caught him behind the ear.

The Killmaster moved in, but he didn't count on the other man's skills as a matador. Torres feinted and got an elbow in Carter's throat. The Killmaster staggered back, gasping for breath.

Out of the corner of his eye he could see that the others had drifted from the main house. They stood now, silently watching.

Torres danced in slowly, sure of himself. His eyes were steady, his face showing nothing.

Carter waited until he was close, and made his own move when Torres swung. Carter grabbed the outstretched arm and twisted it with every ounce of strength he had. He got it behind Torres and pulled upward on it. Then he chopped the Spaniard on the neck with his free hand and Torres went down, face first, into the dirt.

He got up quickly, choking for breath, his face full of

mud, and made a lunge. Carter brought his knee up quickly and caught him in the pit of the stomach and, when he slumped over, chopped him on the neck again.

He lunged at Carter from a sitting position. The Killmaster sidestepped and let him fall headlong into the grass and mud, straddled him quickly, and rapped him a half-dozen times on the neck. Paco turned blue and began to struggle for breath, then slumped out cold.

Carter turned to the others. "Drag him inside and clean him up. We get back to work in an hour."

All that day he worked them hard, Torres especially. By nightfall, all of them were too dead tired to think about anything but bed . . . alone.

The next day was no easier. That night Carter went over the escape plan, detail by detail, and had each one parrot back his part in it.

"Paco, after you've nailed the two in the television monitor room, get to the parking area. I want every car except our Bentley and one other out of commission. Is that understood?"

"*Sí.*"

"Tommaso, the Bentley is in place?"

"It is in the parking lot of the bank in Pau."

"We'll drop you, Lola, and Paco off there. Paco, does the suit-of-lights costume fit you?"

"Tight, but, yes, it fits."

"Gabin, the cars you rigged in Avignon . . . they are placed?"

Fullmer nodded. "They are in a deserted barn outside the village of De Flores. It's about four miles from the frontier over the mountains."

Carter smiled. "That means we have a twenty-seven-mile stroll tomorrow. We leave at first light. I suggest everyone get a good night's rest."

SIXTEEN

It was a cold, clear, crisp night with a big moon hanging above the Château Charmont. Its light created a kaleidoscope of shadows over the house and gardens.

From his position on the hill nearly a mile away, Carter noted the arrival of every car. He counted the number of people, and noted if there was a chauffeur.

All had gone well during the crossing. They had picked up the two cars—a Citroën and a large Renault—and driven on to Pau. There, Lola and Paco and Tommaso had gone their own way in the Bentley.

In the Citroën and Renault, they had driven hard all day and hidden the cars again in Montpellier. From there they had taken buses and the train on into Arles, as if they were mountain hikers returning from a Pyrenees vacation.

Separately, they had hiked from Arles to the hillside where they had rejoined at dusk.

The only remaining part of phase one was the kidnapping of Manolo, which would trigger the phone call that would send the Bentley on its way. It was nearly eight o'clock and it had not yet arrived.

"Three got out of that last one," Arturo reported softly

157

to Fullmer. He lowered the binoculars. "One woman, two men."

"Chauffeur?" Fullmer asked, marking down the count.

"Just one," replied Arturo, and studied the house again.

"What's the count?" Carter asked Fullmer.

"Thirty-eight men, forty-seven women."

"There will be many more than that. Twice that many at least," Carter said.

"Only ten chauffeurs so far. Most of them are driving their own cars."

"Jesus," Caylin suddenly breathed. "An Arab and four flunkies in the sweetest-looking Rolls I ever saw!"

"Those are the bodyguards," Fullmer said. "Check what they are wearing so we can check them out later."

"The big guy's in those funny white Arab robes, the others are in tuxedos," Caylin replied, eyes on the gate, looking through the binoculars.

"That car will be bulletproof, if I know my Arabs," Carter growled. "I suggest we use that one to make our getaway from the villa."

"Arturo," Fullmer hissed, "make a note where they park it."

It went on like that, cars arriving every few minutes, until the asphalt parking area and much of the lawn down to the river was heavy with cars. Eventually they were using even the open area between the woods and outside the fence.

In the villa garden, the mass of people were milling around the tables, and it wasn't too difficult to single out the guards by their stiff posture and slow, deliberate movements around the buffet tables. Music from two orchestras filtered up, and the laughter and the tinkle of glasses caressed the night and complemented the music. For a half hour after ten there had been no new arrivals.

And then Arturo piped up from the far left. "They're

here. Tommaso just let Lola and Paco out in the front, and now he's parking the Bentley.''

Carter sighed with relief and checked his watch.

It was nearly 10:40.

The first—and worst—part for Lola and Torres was being greeted by the host, René Charmont. They both passed with flying colors and moved to the center of the party in the great room on the second floor.

There were about seventy-five people in the wildest costumes imaginable milling and sipping cocktails. Even so, Torres in his suit of lights stood out. As Manolo, his costume wasn't part of the masquerade and he drew a crowd at once who knew he would be in attendance.

Torres was obviously nervous. ''Easy,'' Lola whispered, squeezing his elbow. ''Just be your usual conceited, egotistical self.''

There were few Spaniards in the group. Most of the men had grown fat with age and wealth, and the women were fair-haired and light-skinned no matter what their age.

Torres shook hands with the men and bowed galantly to the women as either Solange or Charmont introduced him. Lola, as befitted her station, was ignored, which suited her just fine.

''Bloody awful sport,'' said one oafish man who trickled champagne down an astronaut's suit when he drank.

A plump middle-aged woman dressed as Madame de Pompadour brazenly ran her hand along Torres's thigh. ''How in the world do you get into those?'' she asked in terribly pronounced Spanish.

Torres stared insolently at her heavily embroidered gown, which was cut to reveal masses of powdered flesh. She wore pendant earrings of diamonds and enormous emerald rings on both her hands. As his eyes went from one adornment to another his grin grew wider.

"The same way we get out of them, señora. With help."

The woman giggled and Torres guided her toward the stairs.

Lola shook her head. The matador in his stolen suit of lights was starting early. But there was nothing she could do about it.

She evaded several interested men and drifted out to the flower-bedecked enclosure over the pool. By the time she had come back in, she had placed six of the small plastique charges. She planted two more on the first floor, and the final three on the second. By the time she reached the massive great room on the third floor where the gambling tables had been set up, it was after eleven o'clock.

Carter raised the walkie to his lips and depressed the button. "Arturo, are you set?"

"*Sí*, right on the edge of the river."

"Caylin?"

"I am directly opposite you, ready to go."

"Prepare yourselves to move in," Carter said, and turned to Fullmer. "Ready?"

"All set."

"Berets and masks," Carter said.

They slipped on the berets and pulled them low over the black makeup they had applied to their faces earlier. Then they tied the masks and slipped on the thin gloves. Fullmer carried the nylon rope ladder slung in even coils over his shoulder. Carter slung the lines with the rubber-tipped grappling hooks over his shoulder. Both of them carried shotguns.

Again Carter raised the walkie. "Synchronize watches . . . on the mark it will be exactly eleven-forty." He watched the second hand climb around to the top of the face. "Mark!"

Somewhere in the night, Arturo slipped into the river. On a hill nearly a mile and a half away, Caylin would be moving down through the trees toward his part of the fence. Inside the compound, Tommaso would be setting the rest of the chauffeurs up in the servants quarters.

Carter and Fullmer went down their own hill, jogging in the darkness. When they reached the woods adjacent to the property, they slowed. Emerging from the trees, they moved between the cars parked outside the fence.

"Here," Carter said, dropping to the ground twenty yards from the fence.

It was five minutes before midnight.

There was a burly guard at the bottom of the stairs in an ill-fitting tuxedo. Lola had already tried to lure him from his post with her eyes and her swaying body. He would have none of it.

Traffic in the hall was light. She moved down to the nearest bedroom where she could watch the guard and the stairs, and darted inside.

An obese man dressed in a ridiculous harlequin costume snored loudly on the bed. He reeked of wine.

Lola shook him. When there was no response, she patted him down until she found his wallet. It contained twenty thousand francs. She pushed the largest of the bills into her bodice, slipped a diamond ring from his little finger into her pocket, and, humming, moved back to the door to watch and wait.

Torres's body was bathed in sweat and his hands were shaking as he worked the two picks into the locks. There were few locks in the world he couldn't master, but this one was proving troublesome.

Finally the last tumbler clicked open and he was in the

room. Quickly he pulled open the massive panel of the alarm system and frantically searched through the maze of wires. At last he found the three Fullmer had told him about, and jammed the cutters into the panel.

"Shit!" he hissed.

He had cut one of the power-feeder lines as well as the three to the main alarm. It dangled, spitting sparks each time it hit the steel casing.

He cursed again, then drew the stun gun from beneath the red sash at his waist and rushed up the stairs.

It was midnight.

As Carter and Fullmer crouched, watching, the dock lights at the river went out. A second later the rear terrace and the lights in the pool enclosure dimmed and then they too went out.

"The ass!" Fullmer cursed. "He's cut one of the power feeds and it's shorting!"

"Nothing we can do about it," Carter said. "Let's go."

In seconds they were over the fence and running toward the house. Halfway there, they passed Tommaso running toward the front.

"The help is bottled up," he whispered as he went by them.

They ran through the last of the gardens to the side of the château. Carter had the rope uncoiled and divided in his hands the moment they stopped.

"Make it good," Fullmer hissed. "Someone is going to be alerted the minute they find that cut line."

Carter stepped back ten feet from the side of the villa, exposing himself in the light from the gambling rooms, and sent the hook singing around his head for momentum . . . and let fly.

For what seemed an eternity there was silence and only

the whispering of the nylon cord uncoiling at his feet. Then a distant *thump*. Carter swung his weight on it.

It held.

Silently, they began scrambling up the thin ladder. Fullmer's added weight tightened the ladder and made it easy to climb.

On the roof, they hauled the line to the top. Incredibly, Carter had heaved the grappler into the chimney, which he saw was the only place it could have gotten a hold on the slate roof.

They could hear footsteps to their left. Just as they turned, the two roof guards came around the corner of the chimney. Before Carter could even raise his own stun gun, Fullmer's had nailed both of them.

"Well, well," Carter said.

Fullmer chuckled. "The Prussian eye."

Carter went to the walkie. "Arturo?"

"I saw you go up. I am alone here, five guards, *poof.*"

"Good," Carter whispered. "Close and lock the side gates. Caylin?"

"I'm at the guards' quarters. I'll wait for Arturo and take them."

"Check," Carter said. "Gabin, let's find the trapdoor!"

Torres threw the snap lock on the inside of the television room and, with one last look at the two unconscious men on the floor, slammed the door shut.

He sprinted back toward the front of the villa and almost ran into two men in tuxedos.

"I am sorry, monsieur, no one is allowed—"

That was all he got out. Torres zapped him and got the other one just as he was pulling a Beretta automatic from under his coat.

Torres stuffed the Beretta into his sash and ran on.

• • •

In the rear corner overlooking the garden, Carter and Fullmer found what they were looking for. It was locked from the inside, but with the flat steel jimmy tools, they pried it open. The door came up and Fullmer slipped inside instantly, dangling his feet into the dark hole and disappearing into the darkness. Carter slipped in after him, found the ladder, and lowered the trap.

Carter's flash revealed a bare storage room with a few trunks, dressmaking dummies, and dust a half-inch thick covering forgotten oil paintings. The music and laughter from inside the house were more distinct now.

They found a door and opened it slowly. Steps in a dimly lighted stairway led down to a second door. They went down carefully.

Fullmer eased the door open onto a long, wide hall separating bedrooms. The music and the noise of the gambling rooms hit them solidly now. They could hear the croupier's call and the light click of dice and wheels.

"Down there, the stairs," Carter hissed. "I'll take this end."

In the one-piece coveralls, sneakers, black berets, black makeup and mask, they looked like two grotesques padding down the hall. Fullmer passed a door just as it opened. An enormous fat man stepped into the hall and immediately began roaring with laughter.

"Bloody marvelous costumes!" he shouted.

Carter zapped him with a stun gun and pushed him back into the bedroom.

In the shadows at the top of the stairs, one on each side, they crouched in the darkness. Again Carter brought the walkie to his lips.

"Regis, Arturo . . ."

Caylin's voice came back. "We nailed only ten guards

in their quarters. That means there will be a bloody lot of them floating in the house."

"Can't be helped," Carter replied. "Both of you get set at the pool and terrace exits. Tommaso?"

"*Sì*. We now have two sleeping guards at the front gate, and it is locked."

"Good," Carter growled. "You take the front door and come in at the first charge. Regis, Arturo . . . you do the same."

"Check," came the reply from all three of them.

Carter checked his watch. "In ten seconds, we move."

Tensely, they waited, Carter glanced at Fullmer and nodded. The other man stood up with a stun gun in his right hand and the shotgun in his left, the butt balanced on his hip.

Carter did the same. "You go right to the center of the room. I'll take the bottom of the stairs. Use the shotgun right away, to let them know we mean business."

"Check," Fullmer replied. "And good luck."

Carter hit the red button on the small "send" unit attached to his belt. Two seconds later the first charge went off somewhere on the terrace. Almost at once the screaming began.

"Here we go," Carter said into the walkie, and released the button.

Together, they started down the stairs.

SEVENTEEN

Carter had guessed almost perfectly. Seconds after the first charge went off, René Charmont and the tall, beautiful Solange rushed up the stairs from the fourth floor. Without pausing for a breath, they ran toward the guard and the door he protected.

Pulled along by Solange, almost reluctantly, was Bella Arksanova.

"What is it, Monsieur Charmont?" the guard cried.

"A robbery," Charmont replied breathlessly, "a stupid robbery! Close the doors behind us—"

Before Charmont could finish his orders, Lola was in the hall, running toward them, screaming her head off. Her purse was draped over her shoulder, the stun gun hidden in her right hand by the ruffles of her skirt.

"My God, we're going to be killed . . . we're all going to be killed . . ."

The guard whirled, a 9mm Beretta in his hand. For a second he was stunned by Lola's hysterics.

It was just long enough. Lola triggered two jolts into his body, sending him through the open door into the stairwell. She halted four feet short of Charmont, with the gun covering him and the two women.

"Through the door and up the stairs," she said in a quiet, modulated voice. "Any try for me and you get what he got, in spades."

Solange was cool, almost defiant, but she moved. Charmont was visibly agitated as he followed his mistress, but Lola could tell that his mind was working, slowly figuring out the situation. She wasn't sure, but she thought she saw a faint smile on the Russian woman's face.

Lola was just through the door when she felt a gun muzzle bore into the small of her back. She turned her head just far enough to see Paco Torres out of the corner of her eye.

"So I was right, huh, partner? The real profit is on the fifth floor."

"You ass . . ."

"Give me your gun. The automatic I have in your back is real. It won't stun you, it will rip your spine apart."

Lola had no choice. She handed over the gun. They were at the top of the stairs now.

"What is the procedure, partner? Lock the bottom door and wait for your lover?"

Lola decided it was best to go along with him and let Carter handle it. She nodded.

"You, rich French pig, close the bottom door!"

Charmont punched a sequence of numbers into a telephone-type keyboard on the wall, and the door below them closed with a whooshing sound.

"Now, in there, all of you. Sit where I can watch you!"

They did as they were told. Torres ejected the stun mechanism from Lola's gun and tossed it into her lap. Then he took a chair just inside the door.

"Now we will wait," he said, and added a satisfied chuckle.

They were nearly at the bottom of the stairs before they were spotted. A stout woman turned away from a small knot of people and stared at Carter. She opened her mouth to scream, but nothing came out.

Fullmer was halfway across the room before a few people realized and started shouting. The others stood with quizzical, almost amused expressions, as if the two men with guns and in outlandish terrorist costumes were part of the entertainment.

The charges had all gone off by then, and their noise was being replaced below by the booming roar of shotguns.

"This is a robbery!" Carter shouted. "Everyone against the wall, men on this side, women over there!"

The group before Carter who had been hesitating now understood. The scream finally erupted from the stout woman's mouth and all hell broke loose.

Nearby, a guard in a tuxedo went for his gun. Carter stunned him and he fell to the floor like a rock. The others surged forward.

"Get back!" Carter shouted, and emphasized it by pumping two rounds from the shotgun into the chandelier.

It worked like magic. The crowd in front of Carter parted, the men one way, the women the other.

There was more gunfire from downstairs. Screams and the sound of running feet filtered through the chatter in the huge gambling room. Seconds later, people surged through the side and end doors, their hands high in the air. Without being told they separated by sex and joined the others in the room.

The majority fell strangely silent, staring at Carter with wide-eyed fascination.

"This is a robbery," he repeated. "We want cash and jewelry. If there is any resistance, we will use these." He waved the shotgun.

A tall, immaculately dressed man with gray hair and a walrus mustache stepped from the crowd and strolled toward Carter. "You wouldn't dare shoot . . ."

Carter stunned him and he toppled forward. Blood from his nose ran across the floor, shocking the others into silence and compliance.

"The château is surrounded. All the telephone lines are cut, and the guards, chauffeurs, and other servants have been locked away. Do as you're told and no one will get hurt."

"Line up!" Fullmer bawled from the other end of the room. "Men to the right, women to the left. Move!"

Arturo, Tommaso, and Regis Caylin spilled into the room behind the stragglers. All three smiled when they saw the docile, glittering group.

Caylin trotted to Carter. "The outside is completely secure."

"All right, let's get to work."

With Fullmer at one end of the room and Carter at the other, the remaining three started down the lines with plastic bags. When they were moving well, Fullmer opened his own bag and scooped vast amounts of currency into it from the gambling tables.

"Don't forget the drawers," Carter said.

"Got 'em," Fullmer replied.

Tommaso was approaching a tall, heavily bejeweled, smoldering woman. Just as he stopped in front of her, she ripped off her rings and the emerald necklace she wore and thrust them down the front of her dress. She screamed an oath at Tommaso and stared at him defiantly.

The stocky Italian reached out and caught the top of her gown. With one hard yank he ripped it to the waist, exposing her hard-tipped little breasts and flat belly.

The jewelry clattered to the floor and Tommaso scooped the precious pieces into his bag.

By this time Fullmer had reached Carter's side. "Keep it moving," the Killmaster murmured. "I'm going up and see if Charmont's safe is bulging."

"Check."

Carter charged up the stairs and down the hall to the paneled, steel door. He jabbed the button to the intercom system and, when it buzzed, spoke: "It's me."

He waited ten seconds, and when nothing happened, he punched the button again. "Open up, dammit!"

The door whooshed open and he charged up the stairs. The moment he hit the elaborate, high-ceilinged office he knew something was wrong. It was in Lola's eyes, the way they seemed to stare right through him.

But he put it together a millisecond too late.

"Slowly, señor, bend over and put the shotgun and the stun gun on the floor."

Carter froze. He started to turn, but stopped when the automatic in Torres's hand roared and a slug tore into the carpet an inch from his sneaker.

"Do as I say, señor, or the next one will be in your back."

"You're a fool," Carter snarled.

"I do not think so, señor. You and the *puta* are after the big money. I think I will cut myself in for a slice of it."

Charmont piped up. "There is a hundred thousand American dollars in my safe. Take it and go!"

"That will do for a start," Torres said. "The guns, Señor Boss."

"I'm warning you," Carter growled, "this is too big for you."

"I spit on your warning. It is bullshit. Do as I say!"

Slowly, Carter leaned forward and gently placed both guns on the carpet. As he moved, his eyes met Lola's and blinked.

She came slowly off the chair so as not to alarm Torres, only distract him. "All right, brave one, you win . . ."

"Sit down, *puta*!" The Beretta wavered between her and Carter.

"There is much money . . ."

Carter tensed his right forearm. The spring in Hugo's chamois sheath activated and the hilt of the eight-inch stiletto settled into his palm.

His movement was smooth, not fast, just even. He came halfway up, turning at the same time.

Lola was still four steps away from Torres. There was just enough room. The gun was coming back to Carter when his arm whirled outward from his body.

The gun dropped to the floor when the blade hit Torres in the neck. His hands came up to grip the hilt, but they never got above his chest. He was dead before he hit the floor.

Both Solange and Charmont dived for the desk. Lola had already retrieved the Beretta.

"Don't."

They stopped as one.

"Where's the safe?" Carter growled.

Charmont went too willingly to a shelf near the bay window. He removed several books to reveal the safe.

Carter didn't expect to find anything, but he had to go through the motions. "Open it!"

Charmont opened the safe and stepped aside. Carter rifled it, pulling out letters and documents. There were two heavy bundles of cash and a diamond ring the size of his thumb. These he tossed on the desk. Lola promptly stuffed them into the pockets of her skirt.

"Where are they?" Carter said.

"You have the money," Charmont said.

"The documents," Carter hissed. "The Brandeis documents you had hijacked from the courier in England."

Charmont's jaw dropped and his eyes grew wide. "You are intelligence. The robbery is a sham."

"Smart," Carter said, slapping him a ringing blow across the face. "Where are they?"

"Go to hell, monsieur."

Carter punched him twice in the gut and he fell to the floor, gasping. The Killmaster crossed to Torres's corpse and pulled the stiletto free. He wiped it clean and returned to Charmont. Gingerly, he put the razor-sharp point an inch up Charmont's right nostril.

"When this goes into your brain, you'll never feel it."

"False bottom in the safe . . . second combination," Charmont stuttered.

Again, Carter thought, too easy. "Open it."

The documents were there, all in order, neatly clipped in the same Brandeis folder that had held them when they were lifted.

Carter took them to the fireplace. One by one he wadded them up and tossed them in. Then he lit the pile. As it burned, he watched Charmont and the two women's faces.

Bella Arksanova suddenly looked like death. She hadn't expected this.

Even more interesting was the look that passed between Charmont and Solange. That told him a lot.

"So much for the originals. Now, Charmont, where are the copies?"

"Copies . . .?"

He was a lousy liar and the sudden spark in Solange's eyes told Carter that she was part of the deception. Carter took the Beretta from Lola and pointed it at Charmont.

"The copies."

"I swear . . ."

Carter shot him between the eyes and turned to Solange. He put the muzzle of the Beretta under her chin.

"Where?"

She didn't hesitate. "Microfilm, in his teeth."

Carter slipped the double dentures from Charmont's sagging mouth and placed them on the desk. Then he cracked them with the butt of the Beretta. The back molars shattered, revealing a pencil-thick twist of dark film.

"Bastard son-of-a-whore!" Bella Arksanova hissed in Russian. "He was going to sell them twice!"

"Kind of looks that way," Carter said, turning to face her. "Where's the gold certificate?"

"What?"

"You had to bring it. Charmont was never going to get it because your husband knew I was going to lift the documents before you could make the exchange. But you had to bring it to show Charmont good faith."

She stood, tight-lipped and stoic.

It was Solange who told the tale. "It is rolled into the sash around her waist."

"Stupid bitch!" Bella hissed.

Solange shrugged. "You were going to cheat us."

Carter unrolled the sash and passed the gold certificate to Lola, who jammed it into her purse with a smile. He picked up the stungun, pointed it at Solange, and put her on the floor.

"Let's go."

"What about him?" Lola asked, nodding toward Torres's body.

"He has no identification, and it will be at least twenty-four hours before they can check his fingerprints."

Carter grasped Bella Arksanova's arm and pushed her in front of him out of the room.

"What are you doing?" she cried.

"Taking you with us. You're going to play out this little charade right down to the last scene."

The looting had been completed by the time they reached the third floor.

"We're ready," Caylin said.

Carter nodded. "We'll have to use the shotguns on the tires of as many cars as possible."

"Torres?" Fullmer asked.

"Yeah," Carter said. "He got greedy."

"Where is he?"

"He didn't make it. Let's go!"

They descended the stairs as a group. They were heading toward the cars before it dawned on the others that they had an extra passenger.

"Why the woman?" Tommaso asked.

"I decided we may need a hostage."

The upstairs rooms erupted into screams of hysteria when the guests realized that their attackers were gone. This abated a little when Carter and the others started shooting out the tires on enough cars to bottle up pursuit.

Tommaso appeared with the Arab's Rolls. Arturo was close behind them with the Bentley. They split up between the cars, with Carter shoving Bella Arksanova into the Rolls between himself and Lola.

In seconds the two cars were screaming past the château.

"Slow down a little," Carter said. "Don't forget, we want them to spot the cars and the license plates."

"*Sì,*" Tommaso said, and almost idled the Rolls past the white faces in the windows.

No one said a word as the cars swung through the gates and speeded up.

"You know the route, Tommaso."

"*Sì,* all back roads to Montpellier."

Carter grunted and opened the bar in the Rolls. He took a good pull from a bottle of expensive brandy and, smiling, held it up to the Russian woman.

Her face was colorless in fear and her lower lip trembled as she shook her head to decline.

On the other side of her, Lola was staring at the gold certificate and muttering.

"Shit, oh shit, oh shit, shit, shit . . ."

EIGHTEEN

Outside Montpellier, they switched to the Citroën and Renault. Both cars had been rigged with police and military band radios. These they switched on as they dumped everything that had been used in the robbery into the Bentley.

When the two big cars were well hidden, they hit the road again. On the walkie, Carter instructed Caylin and Fullmer in the back seat of the second car.

"Lola and I have our share from the safe. It's more than enough. Split the cash into four equal shares and load your money belts."

"Right," Caylin replied. "And Torres's share?"

"He has no share," Carter growled. "Split the jewelry into four shares as well, and bag it. I'll explain about it later."

"Check."

They had cut east and were running parallel to the high ranges of the Pyrenees that hid the tiny country of Andorra, when the first bulletin came over the police radio.

The alert was for ten men. There was no mention of any women. Paco Torres was listed as dead under the name of the Spanish matador, Manolo. It was assumed that the thieves were escaping in a Bentley and a Rolls-Royce, and were headed for the frontier crossing at Port-Bou on the Mediterranean coast.

Carter smiled. They hadn't found the Bentley and the Rolls yet, and the assumption was normal that they would go out either by sea or over the frontier at Port-Bou. It was the fastest exit route south from Arles.

So far, he thought, so good.

They hurtled on through the night, passing through sleeping villages without any incident.

It was getting lighter as they approached the outskirts of Laruns, where they would turn south and start climbing into the Pyrenees. Tommaso slowed to drive through the narrow streets. Here and there a light revealed an early riser, but it would still be a good hour before the first light of dawn. Then they were through and starting to climb.

A flash of lightning cracked across the sky, followed by a distant roll of thunder. And almost at once, unannounced, strong gusts of wind scooped up snow from the side of the road, blasting the car.

It began to rain, slowly at first, the big heavy drops of water splashing on the windshield. They were less than twenty miles from the Spanish border when the storm broke powerfully out of the east and threw itself violently onto the road.

"This will turn to snow closer to the top," Tommaso said.

"I know," Carter replied. "More speed. We'll take advantage of it."

"Anything you say, signore," Tommaso chirped from behind the wheel. "Hang on!"

They raced through the whiteness, slipping and sliding on the narrow, dangerous roads.

Another bulletin chattered over the radio. They had found the Bentley and the Rolls. It was assumed that the thieves were now trying to escape by sea, and all available boats and planes were combing the French coastline from Canet-Plage south to the Spanish frontier.

"Caylin?" Carter barked into the walkie.

"Here."

"How far?"

"About four miles."

"And the cart road?"

"About two hundred yards to your right," Caylin replied.

"I see it," Tommaso said, and they swerved into the rutted lane.

A mile later the snow was too deep for the cars.

"All right," Carter said, "this is it. From here we walk. Break out the parkas and the snowshoes."

"I will go no farther!" Bella Arksanova exclaimed.

"You'll go," Carter said, "or I'll shoot you where you sit."

She climbed out of the car.

Caylin led the way along a narrow cart track. The going was slow. By Carter's watch it was nine o'clock, and they had covered only a couple of miles.

The storm was reaching its peak. It was difficult to see more than a few hundred yards ahead. The wind whistled and drove the snow into their eyes and faces with stinging ferocity. Carter didn't know how many times he fell to the ground and pulled himself back up, only to be staggered by the wind. Heavy black clouds raced across the sky and seemed close enough to touch.

Full light and the sky was black. There was no way of telling whether they had crossed the border. The rocks rose around them in an impossible barrier. Countless times they passed along the trail beside dropoffs of more than a hundred feet, and after that, the snow closed in and left the imagination to dwell on what lurked below the impenetrable mists.

Suddenly they stopped and Caylin made his way back to Carter.

"We are over the frontier now," he said. "Here the trail splits. The right fork leads directly down to my ranch. It is dangerous."

"How far?"

"About twelve miles. It is the way I planned to go, but I didn't count on the storm."

"What's to the left?"

"A small village, Contalet. There might be a car there we could buy or rent to take us to the ranch."

Carter stared directly into the other man's eyes. "Regis, we're not going to the ranch."

"What?"

"I have reason to believe that we will have a welcoming party there. You may not be able to go back to your ranch for several weeks, maybe never."

Caylin stared at Carter for a long moment, and suddenly shrugged, patting the money belt inside his parka around his waist.

"The property is leased anyway, and I am due for a long holiday."

"Good man," Carter said. "How many trails over the mountains in this area?"

"Four. These two, and two larger ones to the east."

"Tell the others to relax for a bit."

Carter grasped Bella Arksanova by the arm and drew her away from the others.

"There are four trails here down the Spanish side of the mountain. How many of those are being watched by your men?"

She looked away without a word.

"I could take my chances and just strip you and leave

you up here. You'd freeze in a half hour."

She still said nothing.

Carter sighed. "Anything for the cause, eh, Major? Give your all for Mother Russia and have the Red Banner draped over an empty grave?"

She turned and spit at Carter, but the wind carried it away.

The Killmaster took the film out of his pocket and held it in front of her eyes. She reached for it, but he was quicker.

Shielding the flame of his cigarette lighter with their bodies, he touched it to the strip. It sizzled, and in seconds it had disintegrated.

"Now, Major, you have no cause to die for. What's it to be?"

Her shoulders sagged and the fight went out of her. "There is a team of ten men at Caylin's ranch. They are backup. All four of the trails are covered."

"How many men?"

"I don't know for sure. I think six."

Carter left her and returned to Caylin. "We take the left trail to Contalet."

The trail dropped sharply, and about three hundred yards below they could make out the cottages, small buildings, and the spire of a church.

It was Contalet.

"Something's wrong," Caylin said. "It's noon. Even in this storm there should be some activity."

"I've got a pretty good idea what it is," Carter said, passing his Luger to Caylin. "Somewhere down there I'm going to find some wheels. Lola has a Beretta. The two of you cover me, and keep checking behind you."

"And if you get a car?"

"I'll drive it to the end of the village, there behind the church."

"But what then?"

Carter smiled. "You'll see." He started away.

"Wait . . ."

"Yeah?"

"This is not the border police you fear, is it?"

"No, it isn't. But that's not up to you."

Carter took off in a zigzag pattern toward the village.

The truck was behind one of the cottages under a crumbling lean-to. It looked in decent shape with fair tires.

Carter darted a quick look around, then began to slither across the open area. But he never made it. A tall man in a fur coat and hat stepped around the corner of the cottage and leveled an automatic at him.

"Good afternoon, Carter. My name is Orlov. Please cooperate. My orders are to take the documents from you and let you and your group proceed on your way."

Carter moved his hands out from his sides. "I am not armed."

"That is good. Bodies are so messy. The documents, please."

"Orlov, is it?"

"Yes."

"I don't have the film, Orlov."

"Please, please . . ."

"But I do have Major Arksanova."

The surprise on his face was genuine. This new development made his concentration stray just enough.

Carter jumped, got hold of the gun, and held on. It fired wildly. The Killmaster butted Orlov with his head, catching him on the chin. Orlov went down, the gun flying into the snow.

Carter rushed him, swung an intentional wild right, and

jerked back as Orlov tried to block it. He was open in the stomach. Carter hit him as hard as he could. Orlov bent over and landed in the snow, then sprang back up, lunging at Carter. They went down together.

The Rusian had Carter around the throat, riding him with his weight and forcing his face into the snow. No matter what the Killmaster tried, he couldn't free himself and he was having trouble breathing.

Suddenly the weight was gone. Carter rolled to his knees.

Orlov was staggering to his feet. Beside him, Lola stood, a huge hunk of shattered wood in her hands. As Orlov moved, she laid it across his back again, and it shattered completely.

"We spotted him," she said. "I followed you."

"I can see. Where are his friends?"

"Guarding the road on the downside of the village . . ."

Orlov came off the ground like a roaring bull to plant his shoulder in Lola's belly. She sailed, and the Russian scrambled in the snow for his gun.

It was obvious to Carter now that Orlov assumed he was bluffing about his superior's wife. Carter ran at him and kicked him in the face. Orlov went down and Carter kicked him again.

The Russian turned and tried to crawl away, but Carter ran alongside him, kicking him like a dog.

Orlov jumped up suddenly, and lunged, managing to get his thumbs into Carter's throat.

The Killmaster jabbed both hands into the other man's eyes, pushing with all his strength. Orlov released his grip, and Carter tore free. At the same time, he lashed the Russian in the face, jumped behind him, and locked his arms, lacing his fingers in back of the other's neck.

It was the end.

"Quit, Orlov," Carter hissed.

The Russian struggled, kicking backward with his right leg.

Carter tightened his hold. Orlov stomped the ground and tried to throw Carter off his back. The Killmaster hung on, applying pressure. More and more pressure. He pulled back hard, straightening his arms with the last of his strength.

Orlov's neck snapped.

His head fell forward loosely on his chest and he sagged to the snow. His body quivered, his right leg twitched several times, and then he lay still.

Carter sank to the ground, his breath coming in short, desperate gasps. Lola's feet appeared at his side.

"You're all right, aren't you?"

"Oh, hell, yes," Carter wheezed. "I'm Superman. See if the keys are in that damn truck."

He staggered to his feet and moved after her. Just as they reached the truck, an old man emerged from the rear door of the cottage.

"The keys are in the ignition," Lola said.

"Is this your truck, old man?" Carter said. The man nodded. "We're buying it," he said, and turned to Lola. "Pay him."

"With my money?" she squeaked.

"You bitch . . ."

"All right, all right," she said, leaning out the opposite window and shoving a wad of bills into the old man's hand.

Carter started the truck and backed from the lean-to in a swirl of snow.

The truck was behind the cathedral. Tommaso was in the driver's seat revving the engine. Lola sat beside him. Arturo and Regis Caylin were in the rear, behind the sideboards.

Gabin Fullmer was helping Carter lash Major Bella

Arksanova across the grille. With each tightening knot to her wrists and ankles, she spouted a new stream of curses at them in Russian.

"Do you think this will work?"

"If it doesn't, she gets it first," Carter replied. "And my guess is they won't want to answer to her husband for that."

"That does it," Fullmer grunted, tightening the final knot.

"Okay," Carter said, "you get in the back. Those of you with guns, don't use them unless they fire first and we have to shoot our way through." He climbed into the truck. "Tommaso . . ."

"*Sì?*"

"Go slow, very slow. If they don't move the barricade, I tell you when to crash it."

"*Sì.*"

The truck rolled slowly forward.

The tension was so thick it would have required a machete to cut through it.

They couldn't see the KGB agents, but they could spot the snouts of their guns poking from behind trees and over fallen logs.

Tommaso inched the truck forward in its lowest gear. About four hundred yards from the makeshift barricade across the road, one of them fired a warning shot.

"Don't stop," Carter said. "Just keep going slow. They'll recognize her soon."

"*Sì.*"

"Maybe they won't give a damn," Lola said, her voice quivering.

Carter shrugged.

At two hundred yards, they recognized the parka-clad woman draped across the front of the truck. There were shouts back and forth across the road, and one man stood full up to make sure.

"Keep going," Carter said.

At twenty yards from the barricade, Bella Arksanova broke. She started screaming in Russian at the men in the trees. Two of them dropped their rifles and ran into the road waving their arms.

"Stop," Carter said, a sigh of relief in his voice.

Tommaso braked the truck and calmly lit a small cigar.

It took the men fifteen minutes to remove the logs and debris from the road. When they were finished, Tommaso eased the truck through. Five pairs of hate-filled eyes watched their progress.

"Hit it!" Carter hissed.

They careened down the mountain for nearly five miles as fast as the truck would go.

Bella was shouting at the top of her lungs.

Carter leaned out the window. "What did you say?"

"I am freezing! You are freezing me to death!"

"Won't be long now."

He rolled up the window and lit a cigarette.

Five miles later he called a halt and cut her loose. "Strip."

"What?"

"Strip, comrade, down to your shoes."

"I will freeze!"

Carter shook his head. "No, you won't. It's warming down here and the snow has turned to rain. Strip!"

She did, finding new curses for him with each item. When she was stark naked, wearing only her shoes, she started to weep.

"Don't cry, Major," Carter growled. "Just start back up the road. Your friends will catch up with you."

He crawled back into the truck.

"Let's go. Head for Zaragoza!"

• • •

They abandoned the truck in Zaragoza and walked into the center of the city on foot.

"All right," Carter said, calling a halt, "this is it. I suggest you spread in every direction and get out of the country as quickly as you can. The jewelry will be insured. You all know the best deal is to settle with the insurance company. I'd wait about a year. Just figure you're giving yourself an annuity."

In turn they all shook hands.

"You're a fine bunch of honest thieves," Carter said, grinning. "You'll never really know how fine. And, one more thing. If I were you, I would forget all about the Russian you heard back there."

One by one they drifted away. Lola lingered.

"Where to this time?"

She smiled. "I think Rio. I've never been to Rio."

"They'll miss you in London."

She shrugged. "I think it's time Lola went the way of Serena. Maybe this time I'll be Tereza. That's a good name for Rio!" She went to her toes and kissed him lightly. *"Adiós, mi amor."*

She started off and Carter suddenly remembered, patting his pockets.

"Hey, Tereza!"

"Sí?" she said, looking coyly over her shoulder.

"I'm busted. Could you lend me . . . ?"

She took an American twenty from her purse and pressed it into his hand.

"Damn, sure you can spare it?"

She shrugged and laughed. "I figure you'll show up again someday and pay it back."

Carter waited until she had passed out of sight beyond the last streetlight before he turned and walked the other way.

DON'T MISS THE NEXT NEW
NICK CARTER SPY THRILLER

DAY OF THE ASSASSIN

A little snooping and Carter found out that Tall-and-Handsome and Plump-and-Redheaded were Mr. and Mrs. Raymond Justice. He scouted the bar, the beach, and the pool, but he didn't see them.

From the lobby pay phone, he called the desk. "Yeah, put me through to Ray Justice, please—this is long distance. He's in Suite Ten-twelve."

"No, sir, that's Bungalow F. I'll ring."

"Thanks."

The voice that answered had a British accent. "Yes, what is it?"

Carter held his nose. "Room service, Mr. Justice. I think we've got a mix-up here. Did you just ring for cocktails?"

"I did not."

"Sorry."

The Killmaster hung up and went into the concession shop across the way. He bought a can of lighter fluid, pocketed it, and headed out across the pool area. In the gardens he turned right to the row of bungalows that fronted the beach. Bungalow F was the fifth one in a line, and all the drapes were drawn.

Carter hugged the door and knocked.

"Yes?"

"Room service, sir."

The door swung wide. "I just told the chap on the phone—"

Carter nailed him from the side, flush on his right ear, and Justice went to one knee. Carter shoved him back into the room with a foot in the center of the chest, stepped into the bungalow, and closed the door behind him.

The guy was in swimming trunks and he was no shrimp. He bunched the muscles in his big shoulders and came off the floor to ram his head into Carter's gut.

Carter nailed him again, cupping the palm of his left hand across the same ear. The concussive force of the air driven against the eardrum jerked a whistling grunt of pain from the man's throat. His hands came up and his head twisted aside in agony.

Carter stepped in, set his right foot, and buried his fist in Justice's gut. A follow-up left on the point of the chin drove him back against the wall where he folded like a burnt match.

The Killmaster checked the kitchen, bedroom, and bath. No little woman. He found her undies in a drawer and selected a handful of panties, three pair of panty hose, and a bra.

Back in the sitting room, Justice was fighting for air and consciousness.

Carter used a pair of panty hose each on the ankles and

wrists, and attached them. Then he looped the crotch of the third pair around the man's neck and attached it to his wrists in the small of his back. If Justice struggled too much to free himself, he would choke to death.

The panties Carter stuffed in the man's mouth as a gag, and secured them with the bra knotted tightly at the back of his head.

As a last touch, he ripped apart the man's swimming trunks and threw them across the room. A naked man with it all hanging out develops an inferiority complex that sometimes makes him talk faster.

Carter moved back into the bedroom. The man's wallet, his passport, and about two thousand in cash lay on top of the dresser. The wallet said he was Raymond Justice, age forty-one, and according to a driver's license about to expire, he lived in Baltimore.

The passport was a little more revealing. According to the last set of entry-and-exit stamps, Justice had entered Portugal four months earlier and stayed there until only a week ago. There was an international driver's license tucked into the back of the passport, with an issue date on it about two weeks before the entry date on the passport into Portugal.

Back in the living room, Justice's eyes were bulging and his face was darkening from lack of air. Saliva was dripping from the corners of his mouth around the panties and dribbling down his chin.

Carter knelt in front of him and stared at the plea in the man's eyes, the kicking legs, and the straining shoulder muscles.

"Can you hear and understand me? Nod!"

Fierce hatred in the eyes and no movement of the head.

Carter backhanded him, hard, across the face, and the head started nodding as if it were on a string.

"I'm going to take the gag out, but don't breathe. If you

breathe, you'll aspirate into your lungs and have pneumonia by five o'clock. Got that?''

More nodding.

Carter rolled him facedown onto the floor and untied the bra. When he jerked the panties from Justice's mouth, he hit him hard in the center of the back. The results of Carter's gut-punch spewed out onto the carpet and in a couple of minutes the man was breathing normally.

''Oh, God . . . sick, I'm sick,'' Justice gasped.

''Shit, friend,'' Carter rasped, ''you don't know sick yet.''

He rolled the man back to a seated position and again knelt in front of him. ''Where's the little woman?''

''Out.''

''I can see that. Out where?''

''Hairdresser's. Look here, I don't know who you are . . .''

Carter smiled. ''You mean you didn't know who I was until I walked through that door. Now we're going to play twenty questions, and if you want to keep your manhood, you'll answer every one of them right on the nose. We'll start with something easy. Who do you work for?''

Justice lunged forward, trying to butt Carter with his head. The Killmaster twisted aside and jerked his knee up into Justice's face. With a howl of pain and his nose spurting blood, he tried to rise for another go, but he could only get to his knees.

Now Carter decided to really get rough. He laughed aloud, got to his feet, and grabbed a handful of the salt-and-pepper hair. He jerked Justice's face down, and at the same time drove his knee a second time into the handsome face.

''I can keep this up a long time, Justice, so long even your own mother wouldn't know you when I'm through.''

He lifted Justice's head and brought his knee into position to drive it up again.

"No, no, please, enough . . ."

Carter paused with the knee but kept his grip on the hair. "You want to try me again? How about it?"

"No more, no more, please!"

"So you say now. I don't think you're quite convinced."

"You're crazy, a crazy bastard! What do you want?"

"I already asked. Who do you work for?"

"The government, foreign service."

"And you're currently attached to the embassy in Portugal." Justice looked surprised. "Your passport is diplomatic. What brings you to California?"

"Loretta and I are on holiday."

"Loretta's the little woman?"

Justice nodded. "She's a military analyst. We're stationed together at the embassy in Lisbon."

"So far, so good," Carter growled. "What do you do for Comrex?"

"Comrex? I don't know anything about Comrex."

Carter shook his head and gave the man a world-weary smile. "Raymond, my boy, you are so frigging stupid. I'm a pro and you are in over your ass."

The Killmaster gave him a long ten seconds to come up with an answer. When he didn't, Carter got to his feet and walked to the glass doors that led to the rear patio. They were decorated with little butterfly decals so that guests under the influence wouldn't walk through them on the way to the pool.

The bungalows were all top-drawer. Each of them had its own small pool and enclosed patio.

He opened the glass door but left the screen door latched, and returned to Justice.

The man was frightened and bewildered. He was still not actually aware that he was stark naked. Carter dragged him to his feet and across the room. Five feet from the patio exit, Carter sent him sailing through the screened door. The wire parted like bacon sizzling, and Justice sailed end over end across the patio with Carter right behind him.

The Killmaster rolled him over and over with well-placed kicks until the man slid into the pool. He tried to shout, but water filled his mouth, cutting off his cry as he sank.

Carter went to the side of the pool and looked down into the clear water. Justice kicked and lunged trying to fight his way back to the top and life, up where the air was. He made it, throwing his head back, mouth open and gasping. Carter put his foot on Justice's head and shoved him back under.

Twice more when Justice surfaced, Carter let him get just enough air to give him hope, and sent him down again. When Justice quit making bubbles and stopped struggling and came slowly floating to the top, Carter grabbed a handful of hair and towed him facedown, turned his face to the side, then pounded on Justice's back with the side of his right fist. In a few moments Justice stirred, opened his eyes, saw Carter, shut his eyes, and shook his head.

"I'm dying . . . you're killing me . . ."

"Not quite, but almost," the Killmaster hissed. "Who's your immediate superior in Comrex?"

The swollen eyes came up and weighed Carter. They flickered and the jaw set. At that moment Carter knew he wasn't going to get anything substantial out of the man.

"I talk, they kill me. I don't talk, you kill me." He shrugged. "Go to hell."

Wearily, Carter yanked the panty hose tight against the man's carotid artery. In seconds Justice was out cold. He wrapped his hand around Justice's arm just above the elbow, lifted, and dragged him back through the living room into the bedroom.

When the panty gag was back in his mouth and secure,

Carter went over the bungalow again. The only item he unearthed that he had missed earlier was a spare clip for a .25 automatic. Because of the caliber, and the fact that he couldn't find the gun, it was a good guess that it was in little Loretta's purse.

This gave Carter another piece of interesting intelligence. If the lady was packing and her husband wasn't, then it was probably Loretta Justice and not Raymond who had the final order on Carter if they found him.

He got a fresh supply of panty hose and went through the bungalow extinguishing all the lights. This done, he settled back to wait.

It wasn't long, twenty minutes, when he heard the *tap, tap, tap* of her heels on the walk.

He took her just as she came through the door. "Ray . . . did you go back to bed . . . ?"

He wasn't gentle. He flipped a noose of nylon over her head, jammed the knot tight against her neck under the ear across the carotid, and kicked her feet from under her. In fifteen seconds she was unconscious.

He picked her up, carried her into the bedroom, threw her on the king-size bed beside her husband, loosened the knot so blood could get to her brain, and then stripped her.

Each time she seemed to come back almost to full consciousness, Carter tightened the noose and she went out again. He stretched her full length and tied her hands above her head, her feet to the footboard.

He loosened the knot and let her come back all the way, helping her by dumping melting ice wrapped in a towel on her belly. After a moment, he moved the lumpy towel up between her vast breasts and used an end to wipe her face.

She shook so hard with fear, and perhaps with cold, that Carter could feel the bed tremble against his leg. When she looked to her left and saw her husband lying there like a

roped calf, she gasped, slung her head back and forth, and
tried to scream. But nothing would come; all she could
make was a thin whine.

"Can you hear me, Loretta?"

"Wh-who . . . are . . . you?"

"Can you hear? Do you understand?"

"My *God*, what's going on?"

Carter found her purse and lifted the little Beretta .25
automatic from it. It was definitely a woman's gun, but up
close it could be just as deadly as a Howitzer.

He returned to the bed and looked down at her, smiling,
holding the gun above her face with two fingers. "Hi,
Loretta. I'm the guy you were going to use this on."

Her face was already a little gray; now it went stark white.
She took another gander at her husband, gave him up for
dead, and stared back at Carter.

"Want to tell me about Comrex, Loretta? Who gave you
your orders in Lisbon to take a holiday in California? Who
runs you here? That's for starters." He pulled up a chair
and sat beside the bed. "Old Ray over there decided that I
was the lesser of two evils. He told me to go ahead and kill
him. What do you say, Loretta?"

Her eyes flashed. "I am an employee of the United States
government. I don't know who you are, but —"

"Oh, shit, Loretta."

Carter took the can of lighter fluid from his pocket and
moved to the head of the bed. He sprayed her right hand
with the fluid and snapped his lighter until it flamed.

"My God, you're a sadist!" she cried.

"No, Loretta, a realist." He touched the lighter to the
right hand and it immediately burst into flames.

Loretta's back arched and her eyes rolled up, showing a
rim of white. For the first few seconds the yellow flame
tipped with blue didn't harm her, only burned, and she

watched with terrified fascination. Then the excess fluid burned away and the fire began to eat into her flesh. She screamed.

Carter jammed his hand over her mouth. She tried to bite him. He slapped her, hard. He took a handful of panty hose and jammed them into her mouth. He sprayed her hand again and lit it. She bucked and fought the nylon bindings of her own panty hose that tied her to the bed. Carter put the fire out, slapping the flames away with his hand. Her hand was puckered with burn blisters, none serious.

He sat down in the chair and took the wadded nylon from her mouth. "Loretta, I'm only going to say this once. Do you hear me?"

"Yes."

"Then listen. If you don't tell me everything I want to know, I am going to melt you."

For emphasis he emptied the can of lighter fluid over her body, starting at her breasts and moving all the way to her toes. Then he held up the lighter.

"One touch, Loretta, and *poof*, up you go."

—From DAY OF THE ASSASSIN
A New Nick Carter Spy Thriller
From Jove in March 1989

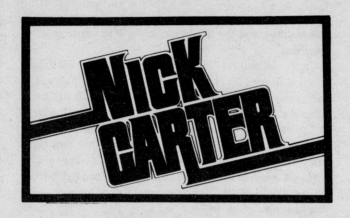

☐ 0-515-09055-7	EAST OF HELL	$2.75
☐ 0-515-09112-X	KILLING GAMES	$2.75
☐ 0-515-09214-2	TERMS OF VENGEANCE	$2.75
☐ 0-515-09168-5	PRESSURE POINT	$2.75
☐ 0-515-09255-X	NIGHT OF THE CONDOR	$2.75
☐ 0-515-09324-6	THE POSEIDON TARGET	$2.75
☐ 0-515-09376-9	THE ANDROPOV FILE	$2.75
☐ 0-515-09444-7	DRAGONFIRE	$2.75
☐ 0-515-09490-0	BLOODTRAIL TO MECCA	$2.75
☐ 0-515-09519-2	DEATHSTRIKE	$2.75
☐ 0-515-09547-8	LETHAL PREY	$2.75
☐ 0-515-09584-2	SPYKILLER	$2.95
☐ 0-515-09646-6	BOLIVIAN HEAT	$2.95
☐ 0-515-09681-4	THE RANGOON MAN	$2.95
☐ 0-515-09706-3	CODE NAME COBRA	$2.95
☐ 0-515-09757-8	AFGHAN INTERCEPT (on sale October '88)	$2.95
☐ 0-515-09806-X	COUNTDOWN TO ARMAGEDDON (on sale November '88)	$2.95

Please send the titles I've checked above. Mail orders to:

BERKLEY PUBLISHING GROUP
390 Murray Hill Pkwy., Dept. B
East Rutherford, NJ 07073

NAME_____

ADDRESS_____

CITY_____

STATE_____ZIP_____

'Please allow 6 weeks for delivery.
'Prices are subject to change without notice.

POSTAGE & HANDLING: $1.00 for one book, $.25 for each additional. Do not exceed $3.50.	
BOOK TOTAL	$_____
SHIPPING & HANDLING	$_____
APPLICABLE SALES TAX (CA, NJ, NY, PA)	$_____
TOTAL AMOUNT DUE	$_____
PAYABLE IN US FUNDS. (No cash orders accepted.)	**112**